W9-BGC-879

"You're not going to win, Bhodi Li . . ."

Mandarr pulled out his phaser and aimed it right at Bhodi's face. "I could kill you right now."

"Go ahead," Bhodi dared him.

Pirarr leaned forward and thrust his grizzled, green face into Bhodi's. "We're going to take you back to Arr with us."

Although he felt inner revulsion, Bhodi remained cool. "You can just forget that."

Mandarr leaned forward. "No. You can remember it. You can remember it as you sit here in this dark, dank cell, while we aid this gentleman here in winning his little war."

Bhodi looked up and his heart froze.

Adolf Hitler stood in the doorway of his cell, staring at him with undisguised hatred . . .

ARMCHAIR "FAMILY" BOOKSTORE
PAPERBACK EXCHANGE—COMICS
OPEN WEEKDAYS 10-9 SAT. 10-6 (SUNDAY CALL)
3205 S.E. MILWAUKIE AVE.
PORTLAND, OREGON 97202 (238-6680)

Berkley Photon novels

THIEVES OF LIGHT
FOR THE GLORY
HIGH STAKES

Most Berkley Books are available at special quantity discounts for bulk pur-
chases for sales promotions, premiums, fund raising, or educational use.
Special books or book excerpts can also be created to fit specific needs.

For details, write or telephone Special Markets, The Berkley Publishing Group,
200 Madison Avenue, New York, New York 10016; (212) 686-9820.

A PHOTON
ADVENTURE
NOVEL #1

PHOTON®
THE ULTIMATE GAME ON PLANET EARTH™

FOR THE GLORY

DAVID PETERS

BERKLEY BOOKS, NEW YORK

To the entire cast
of characters at
Marvel Comics . . . and
the fictional characters,
too.

Photon and Photon logo are registered trademarks of
Photon Marketing, Ltd.
THE ULTIMATE GAME ON PLANET EARTH
is a trademark of Photon Marketing, Ltd.

FOR THE GLORY

A Berkley/Pacer Book, published by arrangement with
Photon Marketing, Ltd., DIC.

PRINTING HISTORY
Berkley/Pacer edition/April 1987

All rights reserved.
Copyright © 1987 by Photon Marketing, Ltd. and DIC Animation City, Inc.
This book may not be reproduced in whole or in part,
by mimeograph or any other means, without permission.
For information address: The Berkley Publishing Group,
200 Madison Avenue, New York, NY 10016.

ISBN: 0-425-09811-7

Pacer is a trademark belonging to
The Putnam Publishing Group.

A BERKLEY BOOK ® TM 757,375
Berkley/Pacer Books are published by The Berkley Publishing Group,
200 Madison Avenue, New York, NY 10016.
The name "BERKLEY" and the stylized "B" with design are trademarks
belonging to the Berkley Publishing Corporation.

PRINTED IN THE UNITED STATES OF AMERICA

1

Kindred Spirit

Wise men say that no one is truly evil.

After all, even so-called villains have a firm belief that what they are doing is right. The greatest conquerors in history often felt they were working for a great cause. Entire races were wiped from existence, and the vanquishers always claimed to have good reasons; the beliefs of the vanquished were "wrong," or their skin color wasn't the right shade. Another popular excuse for villainy was fervent religious beliefs. Holy wars were very popular, and how could anyone involved in a holy war be evil?

One wise man, Benjamin Franklin, once said that treason is a charge made up by the winners in order to hang the losers.

Another wise man, Will Rogers, said he never met a man he didn't like.

All of these circumstances and sentiments suggest that there is no such thing as evil, that good and evil are different perceptions of truth, that there are no good guys and bad guys, but simply "us" and "them." Who is good

1

and bad depends on who is talking and who writes the history books.

Actually, the truth is that wise men don't know everything, and Will Rogers never met the Warlord of Arr.

The Warlord of Arr was evil. Completely, irrevocably and irredeemably evil, and no one on Earth (or off it) could possibly argue it any differently. The Warlord knew he was evil and he reveled in it. Not only did he know it, but his minions knew it as well. His minions were also evil, but comparing the Warlord's evil to theirs would be like comparing the sun's light to that of a flashlight.

The Warlord's home, Scarrcastle, radiated the evil of its master. It hung there in the blackness of space like an ugly mushroom cloud of malevolence. Its walls were cratered, and on its launch pads were ships of death poised to fly on attack missions at the Warlord's command. Yet the ships sat unmoving now. The Warlord's troops were idle. For such inactivity there could only be one reason.

The Warlord was thinking.

In the cavernous throne room at the heart of Scarrcastle, the Warlord contemplated a monitor screen up on the wall. Light images danced across it, and repeatedly one particular man's face appeared on the screen. The Warlord studied him carefully, fascinated. Around the Warlord, his hideous Dark Guard awaited his orders.

They did not dare disturb the Warlord in his concentration, but it was puzzling for them as the Warlord had never kept them waiting so long before issuing instructions. Certainly whatever mission he had for them could not be so drastically different from those before, could it? Surely their mutual goal—the irradication of light from the universe—was the only thing on the Warlord's mind, wasn't it?

The image on the screen froze. The Warlord turned slowly in his great chair and looked at his closest aides. They were six of the deadliest beings in the known cosmos and yet, next to the being pictured on the screen, their capacity for evil was minimal.

As always the Warlord's shadowy form wavered, refusing to assume one solid, identifiable shape. His Dark Guardians had long since become accustomed to this. Although none of them would admit it to each other, each was secretly glad that they could not make out what the Warlord looked like. The sight could be enough to send the unfortunate viewer screaming back into the darkness that spawned him.

"I believe," said the Warlord slowly, "that I have found a being whom I can respect."

There was a low gasp from the Dark Guardians. They stood in a semicircle around the Warlord's great throne, and they glanced at each other in surprise. One of them leaned forward. He had four arms, huge fangs and claws, and skin like sandpaper. His voice rasped through the throne room. "Are you saying, My Lord, that there exists one who is . . . your equal?"

There was a cutting edge to the Warlord's tone. "Do not overstep yourself in your speculations, Warriarr. I mean that I have found one who may actually be worthy to be my second in command. At the very least he could be a valued lieutenant in some of the more far-flung regions. My power is the ultimate in the universe, but even I cannot watch everything, everywhere, at all times."

He pointed to the image on the screen. The face was that of a human male adult. He had a high forehead with thin black hair brushed across it. His eyes were keen and . . . evil. He had a small moustache that did not extend much past the very middle of his lip.

"His name is Adolf Hitler," said the Warlord. "I have been monitoring his activities via light waves from his home planet, a place the natives call Earth."

"Earth?" Warriarr echoed. "I remember Earth. That's the backwater planet Mandarr came from." He nodded to one of the Dark Guardians seated nearby. Mandarr, eyes spitting hatred from within the blackness that surrounded them, made no response to Warriarr's "backwater" comment. "Earth is many light-years from here, My Lord," Warriarr continued.

"Do you have a point to make, Warriarr?" the Warlord said.

Warriarr said, "These light waves you are monitoring . . . these are images from a time long ago in Earth's history. We have no idea whether this Adolf Hitler is even alive. We have no idea how Earth progressed during the time it took for those light images to get within range of us."

There was a deadly silence and Warriarr became increasingly nervous at it. "My Lord," he began.

The Warlord cut him off. "Are you implying that I am fallible, Warriarr?"

"No, My Lord."

"I believe you are, Warriarr. Did you actually think I was unaware of the amount of time it takes light to travel from one place to another?"

"Yes, My . . . I mean, no, My Lord."

Another uncomfortable silence. "What you are saying Warriarr, is that you do not know whether Hitler is alive or dead. I do. He is quite dead. An unfortunate turn of events in a war he was waging. He admittedly made mistakes. There is much I could teach him, given the opportunity."

Another Guardian, a burly, bearded, one-eyed creature, said, "When you are the Warlord of Arr, you can make your own opportunities."

"Quite right, Pirarr," said the Warlord with a touch of approval. Warriarr glared but Pirarr took no notice.

"I have recently completed a time-spanning machine," said the Warlord. The nebulous darkness of the Warlord pointed to a far end of the throne room, and a flat black square, four feet on each side, appeared on the floor. On the ceiling above, a similar black square appeared. Black light pulsed between the two squares. "Essentially, it takes the light beams from distant planets—Earth in this instance—and turns them into tunnels. Conduits, if you will. Not only can I see what is coming out, but I can send things back through.''

"Such as projections, My Lord?" asked Warriarr. The customary practice when dispatching his Dark Guardians was for the Warlord to send three-dimensional images of his aides. They had form and substance, but they could not be killed.

"No," said the Warlord. "I cannot sustain the energy projections through temporal fields. Any of you that I send through must be your actual, physical presences. But this Hitler is worth the risk, however minimal. I will send a squad of you into Earth's past. There you will help Hitler gain dominance on his world. After that I'll want you to bring him here, for I have much to discuss with him." There was a pause, and Warriarr stepped in.

"My Lord, tampering with that which is past . . . with all due respect, My Lord, that is extremely dangerous. The repercussions . . . aargh!"

The other Guardians stared in alarm as Warriarr vanished from his place. Warriarr's screams echoed through the cavernous throne room. They could not see where he had gone, but wherever it was, he was clearly in tremendous agony. After a minute the screams trailed off, but Warriarr did not reappear.

"Warriarr will return," said the Warlord in answer to the unspoken question. "He needed discipline for questioning me. He had become too confident of himself lately to suit me."

The Warlord turned towards Pirarr. "Am I correct in assuming, Pirarr, that you do not share Warriarr's reservations?"

"That would be correct, m'lord," growled Pirarr. Even if he had shared them, he would certainly have kept those reservations to himself.

"Fine. You will head the squad. Take whomever you wish with you."

Pirarr stood and surveyed his peers. "Mandarr," he said, "how'd you be liking a trip back to the homestead, matey?"

Mandarr shrugged indifferently. "As you wish, Pirarr."

Pirarr quickly assessed the others. Dogarr would be a bit too ferocious for a mission like this. But Pirarr needed heavy-duty firepower, which meant Bugarr and/or Destructarr. Together they were devastating, but also difficult to control. The only one who could keep reins on the insectlike Bugarr and the heavily armored, low-brained Destructarr was Warriarr, and he was out of it. "Destructarr," he said finally. "We three should be enough, eh, mateys?"

Destructarr stood. "Just tell Destructarr where to shoot and Destructarr will do the rest," he said.

"You will be arriving in the Earth city known as Berlin," said the Warlord. "You will establish contact with Hitler. You will inform him of our mission—to search the universe for Photon energy that we drain and use for our own purposes. That we will eventually drain all light from the universe, at which point Arr will become all-powerful. I believe that this human, Hitler, can be a pivotal part of our campaign. We may be distantly related. On your way."

The three Dark Guardians raised their arms in salute. "Let the Darkness grow," they intoned, and one by one they stepped into the block of black light. Each time the light surged. Within moments they were all gone, shot back into the era of World War II.

Dogarr swiveled his massive head around. "What did you mean, My Lord, when you said that we may be related to this Adolf Hitler?"

The Warlord said, "Keep in mind, Dogarr, that Earth of that time—and even today, apparently—is not a spacegoing planet. They have never had any contact with us, and they are unaware of the battle currently being waged for the control of Photon energy. Yet Hitler consistently claims to be part of a master race. Would you care to guess what that master race of his is called?''

Dogarr's huge head shook.

If the Warlord ever smiled, it would have been at that point. ''The Arrian race, Dogarr. Oh, he pronounces it slightly differently. He says Aryan, not Arrian. But that is a trifle. It seems, Dogarr, that I may indeed have stumbled upon a long-lost relative. And won't we have a splendid reunion.''

A low, evil laugh filled the throne room.

2

Past Tense

"Christopher! Come! Come here. You'll want to see these."

Chris Jarvis stopped dead at the front door, hand resting on the doorknob. He turned and forced a smile. "I was, uh, just going out." He indicated his dark blue wind-breaker. "See? On my way out."

From the living room couch, Grandpa Lou grinned affectionately at his favorite (and only) grandson. He looked for some reflection of his own features in the boy's face. Chris had a ready smile, a round face, snapping blue eyes and dark hair. He was slim, much slimmer than Grandpa Lou had been in his entire life, and his whole body surged with vitality. No, thought Lou. Not much of himself in there at all. Lou was square-jawed with sparse white hair desperately clinging to his head like mountain climbers perched on Everest.

"I see, Christopher," he rumbled. "I see my grandson whom I never see enough, heading out to see his friends whom he sees all the time." He slapped the sofa cushion next to him, indicating in no uncertain terms that he expected Chris to sit down next to him. With an exaggerated sigh Chris walked away from the door and plopped down next to his grandfather.

Grandpa Lou leaned forward, his gray, buttoned sweater straining to remain buttoned against his belly. He rummaged through a shoe box in front of him that was crammed to the top with yellowing black and white photographs. He pulled out a photo of an army regiment, all standing proudly and looking smartly into the camera.

"Have I ever shown you this one, Christopher?" he asked, holding the photo between his large fingers. Chris had always been fascinated by how large Grandpa's hands were. The only more striking feature about him was the odd way his ears stuck straight out, the lobes never touching the sides of his head.

"Yeah, Grandpa, you've shown me. A zillion times."

"There we were, poised to hit the beach at Normandy. It was D day, you know, the major assault that Hitler never expec—" Grandpa Lou's voice trailed off as he realized that Chris was staring off into space. His tone changed as he asked gently, "Have I told you about D day before, Christopher?"

"Yeah, Grandpa, you have."

"It's not everyone who had a granddad who was actually there when history was being made. Not that we were thinking about making history. We were just concerned about staying alive." He leaned back and smiled. "It was worth staying alive for. When we came home, after the war, receptions we got like you never saw. We were heroes. That's when I met your grandma, God rest her soul. I remember it was at Roseland—I saw her standing there and . . . Chris?"

Chris jumped slightly, surprised more than anything that his granddad had called him Chris instead of the more formal Christopher he usually preferred. "Yeah?"

Grandpa Lou sighed. "Christopher, don't you care anything about history? About where you came from, and what's come before?"

Chris stared down at his sneakered feet a moment and then muttered, "Well, I mean, past is past, Grandpa. History doesn't come back, and I really don't see much reason for thinking about it all the time. It's kind of like, if all you think about is what's come before, then you've given up on what's yet to come. Only the future really matters."

His grandfather waggled a large finger at him. "There's an old saying, Christopher. Nobody ever listens to history, which is why it always repeats itself. Do you know who said that?"

"Probably a history teacher," said Chris.

A flashing light suddenly caught the corner of Chris's eye. The round blue ring on his right hand had just started flashing. Quickly he sat on his hand, covering the flashing orb with his leg, but the movement was too slow. His grandfather stared down at his hand and said, "Christopher, why is your ring blinking?"

"Uhm . . . I got it out of a Cracker Jack box, and it always does that when candy is nearby." He stood abruptly and shoved his hand into his jacket pocket. "Gotta go, Grandpa. Bye."

He spun on his heel, but the old man's strong grip encircled his wrist and pulled the hand, ring and all, gently but firmly from Chris's pocket. He pointed at it and said, "All right, Christopher. What is this little gizmo of yours? Where can I get one? And where are you going in such an all-fired hurry?"

Chris's mind raced, conceiving and discarding half a dozen stories to hand his grandfather. He was truly rotten when it came to lies. And that's when it occurred to him. He shrugged his shoulders elaborately and said, "All right, Grandpa. I'll tell you everything. The flashing ring is an alert from a computer named MOM, located on a far-off satellite world called Intellistar."

Grandpa nodded silently and Chris pressed on. "I have to report to the local Photon game center, where I will be transported to Intellistar, where I will be transformed into a Photon Warrior. Oh, when I'm a Warrior, I go by the name of Bhodi Li. I and the other Photon Warriors have to defend the universe from the encroaching darkness of the Warlord of Arr.''

Grandpa Lou stared at him for a full thirty seconds. Then he finally sighed, released his hold on Chris's wrist and said, "All right. Don't tell me. You kids and your stories. Someone with an imagination like that shouldn't waste his days hanging around with an old man. Take off, Christopher.''

Chris bolted to the front door and, as he opened it, his grandpa's laconic voice came from behind him. "How many years will you be gone . . . what was it, Bonnie Lee?''

"Bhodi Li. And it won't seem like any time at all. When I'm brought to Intellistar, it doesn't matter how long I'm gone. I'm returned to the point in time right after I've left, so it's like only a minute or so has passed. No one will even notice I've left.''

His grandfather stared at the door as it closed behind Chris. "I'll notice, Christopher," he murmured. "But I wonder if you'll notice that I've left.''

Chris got that same "coming home" feeling he did every time that he approached the Photon Center. He chain-locked his bike into the rack, and he grinned, studying the long, unassuming building. It was relatively unadorned on the outside, the only clue to the interior being the word "Photon" with the identifying logo painted on the exterior. Completely soundproofed, there was no hint for the uninitiated as to what to expect upon entering.

Chris walked in and was immediately intoxicated by the familiar surroundings. There was the cavernous lobby with exotic music filtering through hidden speakers. Smack in the center was the information booth and token counter, where players purchased game tokens. Chris didn't need to purchase any at this poiont—he had a drawerful at home and always carried a couple around in his pocket.

Chris glanced up at the second-floor lounge area that led into the observation deck. From the deck nonparticipants could watch the players in action. He remembered the first time he had watched a game before playing, his eyes wide and heart pumping with excitement. He had known at that point that this was going to be his game, his release, his . . . life outside of life.

At the far end was the suiting-up area. An array of red helmets and green helmets sat perched on poles, with battery packs looped around them and Photon Phasers sitting securely in the holsters. Players for the next six-minute round were just suiting up and Chris walked in through the turnstile. With experience born of long practice, he wrapped the thin, surgical-like paper cushion around his head, then picked up a battery-pack belt from a table and snapped it on around his waist.

One of the regular players, already suiting up, spotted Chris.

"Hey, Bhodi!" he called out to Chris. "Just in time! We need one more for the red team to make it six on six."

Chris grinned as he lifted a red helmet off its perch. He slung the battery pack over his chest, then plugged the chest pack into the belt. Then he pulled the Phaser from its holster. He hefted it, enjoying the weight. After all the practice with it, it had ceased to become a separate weapon—instead it felt like an extension of his arm.

As he stepped forward to the computer console, he pulled out his wallet, and from his wallet he removed his passport. It was the size of a standard business card, but laminated, with a "zebra label" for computer identification and his picture for human identification.

Chris was the last player in, as the computer operator without glancing up popped a large bubble from the wad of gum in his mouth and said, "Insert passport." Chris did so, sticking it into the slot. "Name you're playing under," asked the operator.

"Cripes, I was just here two days ago, Morris," said Chris. "Have you forgotten me so soon?"

Morris looked up and raised an eyebrow. "Oh, hi." He didn't need to ask further, but instead inputted a name, which glowed at the bottom of the list of players in a pale green light:

BHODI LI

As the game progressed, Chris's score would invariably jump his name to the top. It always did.

Chris scanned the names quickly, recognized a few other names: Wildfire, Ace, Hotshot, Comet Man, a couple of others of varying degrees of skill. No one who was close to his match, of course.

Chris had his Phaser brought on-line, then stepped through the large double doors into the waiting area. Within moments the red and green teams were herded to the respective opposite sides of the playing field.

Chris had no clear idea of just how large the field was. The arena seemed about half the size of a football field, but that was probably because Chris never ran straight across it. His path across the carpeted arena was always zigzag or some other fancy maneuver, around or under the many hidden alcoves from where he picked off opposing players.

The red team lined up in front of their home goal, as did the green team on the opposite end. The ring flashed impatiently on Bhodi's finger. He was needed urgently. Well, he was hurrying as fast as he could.

Mist filled the arena. Bhodi tensed as a sepulchral voice echoed through the arena and the game began.

Bhodi and his five team members began a concerted dash towards the goal of the green team. Within seconds he stood in front of the goal, a small blue star-shaped light set high in the wall.

Gripping his Phaser firmly, Bhodi Li struck a dramatic

stance, his feet several feet apart, his arms outstretched and his Phaser pointed straight outward. "The light shines," he said.

What had once been a shocking, disconcerting experience now enveloped him. Bhodi Li spotted from the corner of his eye another player taking aim, but he ignored the threat and, sure enough, all the players froze into immobility. At the same moment, a cone of blue light blazed forth, coming from a place beyond the goal, beyond Earth. Bhodi felt a sudden lurching, as if the entire world had abruptly been turned inside out and then tossed into a high-speed blender. He felt himself being drawn up, as if on an express elevator. The Photon Center dissolved into a blur, and his eyes caught a quick impression of a huge black nothingness, punctuated by small dots of light. There was a roar in his head, a huge rush of air and, inexplicably, a kind of popping noise.

He hit the ground, still on his feet, his knees buckling just slightly but quickly straightening. If Bhodi Li had looked into a full-length mirror at that moment, he would have seen little trace of his slim seventeen-year-old form. The Photon energy that surged through him had filled him out. His torso was wider, his arms and legs more muscular. Fast as he was as Christopher Jarvis, Bhodi Li in full bloom was far faster—in a foot race Photon Warrior Bhodi Li would have passed Christopher Jarvis as if Chris were standing still.

"You're late. Again."

At the far end of the great hall in which he had materialized, Bhodi saw a fellow Photon Warrior. Or perhaps fellow was the wrong word, for this was Tivia.

Tivia, like Bhodi Li, was about seventeen. Like Bhodi she was fully decked out in the armor of a Photon Warrior (in addition to the chestplate and power belt, there were protective leggings on their arms and legs). Unlike Bhodi, however, she was a striking young woman, and the nonarmored parts of her body were covered with a dark mesh material, including her neck and face up to the bridge of her nose. Her eyes peered out at him, haughty and mocking.

Bhodi could never decide about Tivia. There had been times when he would have loved to have been able to ask out this truly out-of-this-world female. And other times he would have liked to knock her block off.

But at any time he was more than happy to have this capable Warrior at his side.

"You're always the last one to heed the call," said Tivia with undisguised irritation. "You have no sense of priority."

He grinned widely, because he knew that it would annoy her all the more. "I've heard that before. I just like to make a dramatic entrance."

"Well, you've made it. Come on. MOM is waiting."

Bhodi was about to respond, but Tivia quickly turned her back on him and headed into the inner sanctum.

As Bhodi followed her, he glanced out a port at the endless star field outside. It was still difficult, after all this time, to accept that he was on Intellistar, the home base of the Photon alliance. Intellistar was a huge bio-mechanoid entity, floating in the depths of space. Ships were docked in her (to Bhodi, "its" seemed wildly inappropriate) large bays. Bhodi had long wondered when Intellistar was built or created. It was a question he had never had the nerve to ask, perhaps because he was concerned that the answer would trash every concept he'd ever had about the creation of the universe.

A voice echoed around Bhodi, a voice reminiscent of the free-floating voice from the Photon Center back on Earth. "Come on, Bhodi Li. Hurry it up."

"Don't sweat it, MOM," he addressed the master computer that permeated Intellistar. "I'll be there in plenty of time."

"Time, Bhodi Li, may very well be exactly what you do not have," said MOM. There was no hint of humor in her tone, and the seriousness of it was more than enough to hasten Bhodi's steps to the central briefing area.

Tivia had already taken her seat and was pointedly ignoring Bhodi. The other Photon Warriors were seated and they regarded Bhodi Li with a mixture of reactions.

Leon smiled. But then Leon always smiled, because that was the way his mouth was made, and it was impossible for the seven-foot-tall, (from tip of his nose to tip of his tail), 682-pound Warrior lizard to significantly change his expression. If Leon ever went head-to-head with, say, a bulldozer, Bhodi would have at the very least given even odds, and maybe even leaned a little in Leon's direction.

Parcival shook his head in a "won't you ever grow up, Bhodi Li?" attitude. Parcival, also from Earth, was probably the most mature person Bhodi Li knew, which was odd considering that Parcival was only ten years old. In addition to his Photon armor, Parcival had a portable computer strapped to his back with a small hook-up attached to his wrist. The bespectacled youth was, in addition to being a formidable Warrior, an absolute computer genius.

Lord Baethan did not smile or frown. He was above that sort of useless facial expression. Lord Baethan sat gleaming in his chair, his metallic body catching the overhead light in fascinating ways. Baethan was a cybernetic, a seamless blending of organic life and machine. Baethan was the only one who, when he left his home planet of Celtar to join his fellow Warriors on a mission, made you feel as if he were doing you a tremendous favor. Baethan considered himself above all of them, and better than any of them. This would have annoyed Bhodi more than it did if it weren't for the fact that Bhodi suspected, deep down, that Baethan might be right. With his magical arts and his ability to cast illusions, as well as his strength and agility, Baethan was probably the deadliest Warrior—if not being—in this neck of the universe.

Pike winked at Bhodi. It was difficult to know just what

Pike, or as Parcival called him, "Uncle Pike," was ever really thinking. Only a little taller than ten-year-old Parcival, Pike looked kind of like a fireplug with a large, thick body and thick legs that ended in flipperlike feet. His mouth was so wide and thin that it seemed to encircle his entire head. Pike was the consummate con man. Once Pike, who had been alone against five warriors of Arr, had through trickery convinced the five warriors that they in fact were outgunned by 100 Photon Warriors, all in hiding. Bhodi would trust Pike with his life. He just wouldn't trust him in a game of cards.

Bhodi quickly took his seat, and nearby a monitor screen lit up. A single blue and green planet filled the picture.

"Boy, that looks like Earth," said Bhodi. "Doesn't it, Parcival?"

Parcival frowned and leaned forward. "If I'm not mistaken, that *is* Earth. MOM . . .?"

The super-computer's no-nonsense voice filled the room. "Quite right. That is Earth."

Bhodi, normally easygoing and wise-cracking during their briefings from MOM, felt a great thickness rise in his throat, and he felt absolutely no inclination to crack jokes. "Earth? MOM, has the Warlord launched an attack on . . . on Earth?"

MOM's response was quick and straightforward. "Yes."

Before Bhodi's eyes danced visions of Earth covered in a shadow of blackness, no light seeping through anywhere. He glanced over at Parcival. Although the young computer genius was an orphan, with no loved ones to be concerned about, he was still visibly shaken. Bhodi thought of his mom and dad, his kid sister and his grandfather, his friends and classmates, and he leaped to his feet. "Then what are we hanging around here for? Let's get back home and kick those crumbs all the way back to Arr!"

"Sit down," snapped Baethan. "You're a Photon Warrior now. It's high time you remembered just who you are."

"I remember plenty," said Bhodi hotly. "I remember where I came from, and that means a lot to me. We can't all be as uncaring as you, Baethan."

"That is your misfortune," was the cool reply.

"Leon understands," rumbled the huge lizardlike warrior. "Bhodi Li is concerned. To him, home is all that is."

"Right, right!" said Bhodi excitedly. "MOM, send me back. Heck, you shouldn't have even taken me off Earth in the first place if you knew that was the Warlord's next target."

Tivia snorted. "Oh, absolutely. You would have been a fine sight holding off Warriarr with the toy light gun you humans use in your Photon training centers."

"Oh, yeah, right," said Bhodi. "And I bet you—"

"That is quite enough," came MOM's sharp, electronic voice. "Baethan is right. You are a Photon Warrior, Bhodi Li, as are all of you. You are the last, best hope against the forces of the Warlord of Arr, and time would be much better served if there were less bickering and far greater cooperation. And time, I assure you, is something that we have precious little of."

His interest piqued, Bhodi Li dropped back into his chair. "That's the second time you made a remark about time, MOM."

"Very observant, Bhodi Li. I cannot send you back to Earth, for the true fight is not on your earth."

Parcival's eyebrows knit. "If I'm not mistaken, MOM . . ."

Anticipating his question, MOM said, "I have not contradicted myself, Parcival." Parcival let out a sigh of relief. For MOM to contradict herself would completely shatter the worldview of the young computer enthusiast. She continued, "The Warlord has sent three of his Dark Guardians—Pirarr, Mandarr and Destructarr—back into time."

There was a moment of stunned silence, broken first by

Baethan. "Madness," muttered the Wizard Lord. "Complete madness. He is tampering with forces that could bring the end to all there is."

"Quite true," said MOM tonelessly. "It seems the Warlord has taken a fancy to a 20th-century madman named Adolf Hitler."

Bhodi frowned. "Hitler? My grandfather has mentioned him lots of times. He was in charge of Germany in World War II and . . ."

His voice trailed off. Uncle Pike leaned his rotund body in Bhodi Li's direction and said, "And?"

"And he lost the war. And died, I think."

Tivia's voice dripped sarcasm. "You think? You're not certain. A human being so vile that he actually interests the Warlord, and you can't remember any significant history of him?"

"Hey, I wasn't born yet, okay?" snapped Bhodi. "I can hardly remember what I did last Tuesday. You think I'm going to remember stuff that happened over four decades ago?"

"On my planet every young woman is schooled in the entire history of her planet and people," said Tivia airily. "To know where you're going, you have to know where you've been."

"Well, I know where I'm going," snarled Bhodi Li. "Back to World War II Germany." He paused. "Can you send me there, MOM? All of us?"

There was a pause. "Yes." But she didn't sound happy about it. "The time program that allows me to freeze time on your respective worlds would allow me to send you back into time. It's programming that the Warlord has long sought, and obviously has finally found a way to duplicate. But it is extremely dangerous."

"I'm not afraid," said Bhodi.

"It's not personal danger I'm concerned about. It's all of us. To go back into the past risks undoing the future. It is obvious that the Warlord's plan is to undo the results of

Earth's World War II and place Hitler into a position of power. Should this happen, the chances are virtually nonexistent—to be specific, one millionth of one percent—that you, Bhodi Li, and you, Parcival, would ever have been born. Should that happen, the Photon Warriors will not exist as well.''

Now it was Tivia who leaped to her feet. "That's absurd. MOM, I will not dispute that Bhodi Li has some moderate ability as a Warrior, and Parcival's computer abilities are valuable. But I don't need any man.''

"Oh yeah?" snapped Bhodi. "How about that time on the planet Gruenwald when you almost fell into the lava pit, and my grip was the only thing coming between you and a 500-foot drop straight into french fry city?''

"I would have gotten out of it somehow," said Tivia tightly.

"Or how about when that ravenous Owz on the planet Macchio was ready to turn us into a midnight snack, and Parcival's on-board computer figured a way out of it. Where was your 'I don't need a man' attitude then, huh?''

Tivia glared at him sullenly and then said, "I see your point.''

Bhodi Li blinked in surprise. Tivia had acknowledged that he was right and had backed down—even come as close to an apology as she ever would. He wondered if he, supporting the losing side of an argument, would have had the nerve and class to own up to it. His reluctant respect for Tivia went up by the smallest notch.

"Bhodi Li is indeed quite right," said MOM, "and he has presented merely two examples of how closely woven reality is. For this reason, it is imperative that you go back into time and thwart the Warlord's Dark Guardians in their plans to aid Hitler.''

Uncle Pike had been concentrating, putting all the pieces of the puzzle together, but there was clearly some piece that still didn't fit for him. "MOM," he spoke up, "since the Warlord is in the past but we are in the present, wouldn't the effects of whatever mischief they've engaged in already be known? Wouldn't history have already been changed? How could we even be here?''

"Because, Pike, as always I have frozen time on Earth while Bhodi is with us. As a result, the ripple from the Dark Guardians' machinations would not yet have reached present-day. As long as I can maintain the time stasis around Earth, our present is safe, much like a dam protects a town from the rising waters. But should the dam be removed, the waters would rush over the town and drown it. Such would be the case with Earth—and with ourselves.

"Since disruption of time is so major a concern, I will only send three of you. I cannot risk all of you. And because of the time period with which we are dealing, my computations indicate that the most expeditious method would be to send the most humanoid of you. That would be you—Bhodi Li—and Parcival, naturally, and you, Tivia.''

The young princess pulled herself up regally. "With all due respect, MOM, I wish to go on record as saying that I do not particularly enjoy being lumped together in the same species as the physically inferior human race.''

"Physically inferior?!'' Bhodi stuck his hand straight out and then bent his arm at the elbow. "We'll see who's inferior. Let's arm wrestle for the superior species championship.''

Out of the corner of his mouth, Pike muttered to Leon, "Someday those two are either going to kill each other or marry each other.''

"Bhodi Li,'' MOM addressed him, "am I to assume from your earlier remarks that you are unfamiliar with this period of Earth's history? And you too, Parcival?'' When both nodded with embarrassment, MOM said, "Very well.''

Abruptly the complex microcircuitry that Parcival had in his portable computer (which looked like a cross between a backpack and a video cassette recorder) came alive.

Small activation lights blinked, and there was a brisk but untraceable hum as information from MOM flowed into the portable computer's memory.

It lasted for three seconds, finished after it had barely begun. "I have furnished your computer with all the knowledge I have in my memory on Earth's World War II. You will be able to access the information at your leisure, Parcival. Oh," she added drily, "I also inputted information on the noted World War III in the planet Schechter's own history. At that time Schechter was a planet both socially and culturally similar to Earth. By studying the mistakes they made, you might learn how your own planet could avoid plunging itself into its own World War III."

"Aw, that would never happen."

"Odd. That's what the inhabitants on planet Schechter said, just before they were reduced to dust."

Bhodi Li cleared his throat.

Small round devices abruptly appeared in midair, hovering in front of the surprised faces of Tivia, Bhodi Li and Parcival. They were a bit smaller than an average marble, and were silver.

"Instantaneous translation devices," said MOM. "Each of you take one and then—if you'll pardon the expression—stick it in your ear."

They did so. It lodged just at the entry to the ear canal, like a hearing aid. "It's a modification of the translator Parcival jury-rigged some time back," continued MOM. "It's keyed to your individual brainwaves, so that you will be able to understand the German you're likely to encounter. The other object to facilitate your mission is this." In Parcival's hand there now materialized a cylinder eight inches long, the upper quarter of which was designed to turn in a clockwise direction. "A compact transporter!" said Parcival. "But MOM, the energy sources required to recharge this won't exist on the Earth of that time period."

"Quite right," said MOM. "It's fully charged now, but

you can only use it a maximum of three times. Ordinarily I'd be loathe to send any hardware other than your basic Photon equipment back into the past, but time is of the utmost importance, and it may become imperative for you to get quickly from one point to the other.

"I have to warn you of several things. First, the Warlord usually sends energy projections of his Dark Guardians, but the time travel process requires the actual physical beings to go through. That means physically they pose more of a threat. However, you can still dispose of them in the usual manner—by targeting and hitting their respective power plates. Picture the Dark Guardians at the far end of a rubber band and their power plates anchor them there. Cut the band and they'll snap back.

"Also, keep your contact with the locals to the barest minimum. Time travel is tricky enough without getting intensely involved with the natural inhabitants."

"Hey, I know that," said Bhodi. "I've seen *Star Trek*. I've seen *Back to the Future*. I know what the score is. Let's roll."

"I agree," said Tivia.

Parcival ran a quick systems check on his on-board computer. "I'm on-line, MOM. Ready when you are."

The three Photon Warriors began to see a glow forming around them, a faint cone of pale blue energy. They heard MOM's voice, filled with concern. "We'll be completely incommunicado, because you'll be in a different era. I will not be able to help you in any way, except for my monitoring of the Warlord's castle. If I detect that his three Dark Guardians have been returned, I'll know that you have succeeded. But if they bring Hitler with them, then . . ."

"Don't even say it, MOM," called out Bhodi Li. But he had no idea if MOM heard him, for suddenly the main room of Intellistar lurched away at a ninety-degree angle. He was in a long narrow tunnel filled with blinding color, and the energy of Photon crackled around him. He realized that he was staring in the very heart of the secrets of the universe, and it was not something he wanted to know. He closed his eyes tightly, even though that increased the feeling of dizziness.

He had been falling through the tunnel like Alice down the rabbit hole, and suddenly he picked up speed. Some force was pulling on him, as if he were going faster the closer he got to his destination. He shouted out a name, *"Tivia!"* and then wondered why of all people he had called for her.

WHAM!

3

Timed
Entrance

It took a moment for Bhodi Li to realize that he was sitting on solid ground. No, he decided, his gloved hands feeling the hard surface beneath him. Not just ground. A paved street.

The loud blast of a horn snapped him out of his momentary confusion. Basic instinct took over—when someone is honking at you, get the heck out of their way. Bhodi rolled to one side, his armored plating clacking on the road. He bounded to his feet, Photon Phaser already in his hand out of long habit.

A quick glance detected Tivia and Parcival nearby, also scrambling to upright positions. Then Bhodi saw that the truck had braked to a halt mere feet away. It had a very long back, covered over with canvas, and the entire vehicle was ancient. No, Bhodi mentally kicked himself. The truck was just right for its time. He was the one with the incorrect sense of what should be where.

He turned towards his fellow Warriors and said, "Let's get out of here before we're noticed." But he had barely gotten the sentence out, when out of the back of the truck poured ten German soldiers, each one armed to the teeth. Within moments they had surrounded the surprised Photon Warriors.

Bhodi Li had to remind himself that he was not at a costume party. He was not watching a rerun of *Hogan's Heroes*. The long coats they wore might look ridiculous, the helmets strapped to their heads might appear to have come from a toy store, and their rifles were antiquated compared to the sleek Phasers the Warriors carried, yet there was no mistaking the seriousness of their situation or the deadliness of their intent.

Parcival glanced in Bhodi's direction and mouthed the words, "I think we've been noticed."

"Put up your hands, Bhodi Li," said Tivia through clenched teeth.

"The heck with that! We can take them!" said Bhodi.

"No," snapped Tivia. "If we engage them, someone could get hurt. Perhaps the wrong person. You could wipe someone from your time period out of existence with one misplaced shot."

"I don't misplace shots, but I see your point. We'll go with them and make a break when there's no one around."

Indeed there were already a large number of people around. Citizens of Berlin stopped to stare openly at the strangely garbed newcomers in the middle of the street. Bhodi glanced at them, and he saw in each face the same look: fear. Not of them, he sensed. Fear of life. Fear of existence and fear that any day it might end.

Then he caught sight of one face in the crowd. A woman's face. He saw her for only a fleeting moment, didn't even quite catch the contours of her face. But one thing he did see. There was no fear in her at all. Then she was gone, vanished into the crowd.

From inside the truck the sergeant stepped out. He

scanned the scene—his men surrounding three bizarrely garbed people. "Who are you?" he called out. "Present your papers immediately."

Not realizing that he was replying in the same tongue as he was addressed, Bhodi called out, "Uhm, I think we left our papers in our other pants. How about if we—"

But he got no further. The sergeant pushed through his men now, got a good look at the three people in front of him. His jaw dropped at their audacity, to show up here in the middle of downtown Berlin, virtually in the backyard of the Fuehrer. He glanced at their armaments, and he liked them even less. They would make valuable prisoners, but his gut gave him a bad feeling. He had learned long ago to trust his gut (which was ample).

"American spies," he said. "Obviously parachuted in."

"Obviously," muttered Parcival.

"Potentially dangerous."

"Potentially," said Tivia.

"Execute them immediately."

"Execut—wh-what!?" stammered Bhodi. "Now, wait just a minute. Whatever happened to 'Take me to your leader'?"

The German soldiers spread into a half circle. Citizens screamed and scattered to the sidewalks.

Of one mind, the Photon Warriors linked arms. "Shall we dance?" said Bhodi. Tivia grunted.

The Germans took aim with their rifles and at that moment the Photon Warriors crouched and then leaped. In a spectacular standing broad jump the Warriors leaped straight up and over the heads of the soldiers. Their leap carried them clear over the troop transport truck. Landing, the three Warriors spun and rammed their shoulders against the truck. With a screech of metal the truck fell onto its side and blocked the street. It was a narrow street and the truck blocked the sidewalk as well.

The Warriors turned and began to run. With their weaponry they could easily have overwhelmed the soldiers, but the potential deadliness of their Phasers was simply too great a risk to use in the all-too-fragile past.

As the soldiers struggled to get around the truck that now blocked their path, the door on the passenger side of the truck's cab was shoved open and the slightly dazed driver of the transport hauled himself out up to his waist. He had still been in the truck when the Warriors overturned it, and he blinked, trying to clear his blurred vision. The scene snapped into focus as he saw his comrades trying to get around and over the truck, and he saw the three bizarrely garbed people running with space-eating leaps.

Quickly he unholstered his luger, aimed and fired.

Parcival was just hitting the ground at the bottom of a leap when he let out a yell and staggered. Bhodi stopped dead in his tracks and yelled, "Tivia! Parcival's been hit!" But Tivia had already seen and was backtracking with frantic speed.

Parcival was staggering, sparks flying from the computer equipment on his back. He sagged to his knees, shouting, "Help me! Bhodi Li, Tivia . . . help!"

"Halt!"

From yards away the soldiers were pouring over the truck now, pounding in the direction of the two Warriors and their fallen comrade.

Tivia gathered the stunned Parcival up in her arms as the furious Bhodi Li pulled out his Phaser. "Eat Phaser, creeps!" he shouted at the oncoming soldier.

"Bhodi Li, don't!" shouted Tivia.

"Clam up, Princess!" he retorted, and fired.

Light energy lanced from the Phaser, blasting out a chunk of the street directly in front of the soldiers. They stopped, stunned by the power they'd just witnessed. With quick, staccato bursts Bhodi Li carved out a huge chasm in the street. The Phaser rays sounded like a thousand furious hornets and the soldiers fell back in confusion. Rubble and pavement leaped up in a fine shower of debris and within moments Bhodi Li had rendered the street completely impassable.

Parcival lurched to his feet, somewhat uncomfortable that Tivia had been holding him. "I'm perfectly capable of carrying my own weight," he said briskly.

"Are you okay?" asked Bhodi urgently.

"I'm fine. But I'm off-line. The whole computer is down."

"But that means—"

Bhodi was studying the computer equipment on Parcival's back. There was a gaping hole and Bhodi Li could see the guts of the machinery. What Bhodi knew about computer hardware could fit into a thimble, but he knew that Parcival's gear was a hopeless mess. "Let's not stand around and chat," he said. "We've got to get out of here. They were ready to fill us with holes before they could see what we were capable of. Now that they've seen what our Phasers can do—"

"And whose fault is that?" snapped Tivia.

"Now, listen, you—"

Before Bhodi Li could complete his sentence, a bullet buzzed past his shoulder. The Germans were firing blindly over the rubble, but they were firing nevertheless. Suddenly a small cannister-shaped object came flying towards them.

"Grenade!" shouted Bhodi Li. He started to take aim with his Phaser, but Tivia had already stepped forward. Cradled between her thumb and forefinger was a star blade—a small disk with vicious blades radiating outward, similar in design to a *shuriken*. With an expert snap of her wrist Tivia hurled the star blade. It hit the grenade in midair, a safe distance from them, and the grenade blew up in the air. A few pieces of stray shrapnel buried themselves in Bhodi's armor.

"Let's not stand here and chat!" shouted Bhodi, and with that the Photon Warriors dashed headlong through the streets of Berlin.

Civilians screamed and got out of their way as the three Warriors ran along the crowded sidewalks. Bhodi Li couldn't help but notice the oppression that seemed to hang in the air. They passed dozens of shops that were boarded over, and even places where the boards had been pried off revealing broken windows. Swastikas adorned the doors and sides of many buildings. People peered out from behind shuttered windows and quickly darted back into hiding, as if merely looking at the Photon Warriors would condemn them to death. And perhaps they were right.

High-pitched whistles blew behind them, and they ran again, rounding corner after corner as fast as they could. Since they didn't know the city, becoming lost wasn't a consideration. They darted down one side street so narrow they practically had to run single-file.

The door to an unassuming three-story home was flung open. The gesture of openness was so unusual that it caught the Warriors' attention immediately.

Framed in the doorway was a striking young woman with a glint of defiance in her eye. Bhodi Li recognized her immediately. "Hey! She was in the crowd before!"

"That's nice," said Tivia, tugging at his elbow. "Let's go."

The woman in the door looked up and down the street. At that moment there was no one in the narrow street of small, dirty buildings. She gave one more quick glance, and Bhodi Li realized that she was scanning the windows of her neighbors. She wanted to know if anyone was watching her. But why?

Satisfied, she said tersely, "In here. Quickly." Her voice was like iron. "Quickly," she said more urgently.

The Warriors glanced at each other. "Could be a trap," said Parcival.

"It's the devil we know versus the devil we don't," pointed out Bhodi. "We're not going to be able to dodge soldiers forever. I don't see as how we have much choice."

"You want to know what I think?" said Tivia.

"No," answered Bhodi Li, and in two quick steps he was inside the house. With a fatalistic shrug, Parcival followed him and Tivia brought up the rear, backing into the house, her Phaser out and her keen eyes looking for any sign of pursuit.

She got to the door and she half turned, her eyes meeting the steady gaze of her unexpected savior. They stared at each other for a moment and then Tivia stepped into the house. The woman gave one more glance around and then shut the door with a soft click.

The street was silent once again.

4

Into the Underground

The living room was small but nicely furnished. The simple furniture was polished so brightly that Bhodi Li could see his face reflected in it. There was a large brown circular rug, and in one corner was a fireplace with no wood in it. There were no books with the exception of a copy of *Mein Kempf* in the middle of the coffee table. Bhodi wondered what it was about. Maybe it was a German translation of some popular old title like *Moby Dick*.

A small very old photograph of an elderly couple sat on the mantel. Bhodi then realized that the picture was not old, but actually relatively new. It was just that it wasn't a color snapshot or similar photo.

"Who's this?" he asked.

But the woman had no time for questions. "There's no time for chitchat," she snapped. "Let's go. Up the stairs. Storm troopers or the Gestapo could be here at any moment. Up up up."

She shoved them toward a stairway. Tivia turned and said archly, "I'm not accustomed to being manhandled, thank you."

The woman cocked an eyebrow and tilted her head, making her look like an inquisitive puppy dog. "Are you accustomed to being dead? If you're not, then I suggest you move it or we'll all be able to share the experience."

Tivia let out a little annoyed huff and bolted up the stairs behind Bhodi Li and Parcival.

At the woman's urging they went past the second floor and up to the third, to the very top of the house. The Warriors looked around at the small room. There didn't seem to be much in the way of hiding-place potential here.

There was a hatrack in one corner. The woman took the rack and went to a small closet set in the wall. She pushed aside some coats that were hanging in it and shoved against the closet ceiling. Bhodi stepped in behind her and caught a whiff of her perfume. She smelled like violets.

The closet ceiling lifted up with a creak and Bhodi stared up into inky blackness. The woman said, "That is where you can stay. There is a rope ladder that drops down."

"That won't be necessary," said Bhodi Li with a small smile. He crouched slightly and then effortlessly sprang eight feet straight up into the darkness.

He landed straddling the hole in what was now the floor of the room hidden above the closet. He stared downward through the hole and took a small satisfaction in the surprised look on the woman's face. Bhodi Li was relieved that claustrophobia was not one of his problems. He called down, "Come on up here, folks. This is great."

He backed away from the hole as Parcival and Tivia sprang through the hole. So they could move around and talk more freely, Bhodi Li kicked shut the trapdoor, sealing off the woman and the room below.

Tivia wrinkled her nose. When all three were up there, they could barely turn around. Parcival tried to do so and the computer rig on his back sharply banged Tivia in the small of her back. "Will you be careful, Parcival?"

"Sorry," said the young computer whiz distractedly. "This is obviously a secret hideout for people on the run from the authorities. I'd say," and he half turned to face Bhodi, jabbing Tivia in the ribs, "that our hostess is an old hand at this."

"You may be right," said Bhodi Li. "What say we go down and ask her?"

"Anything to get away from these cramped quarters." She turned to remove the trapdoor and found herself nose-to-nose with Bhodi Li. The jaunty Photon Warrior grinned at his female comrade. "Admit it," he said with a grin. "This is where you want to be."

For an answer she shoved past him, gripped the trap-door by a small circle of rope attached to it and lifted it up. The unlit room immediately became a little brighter.

Their hostess moved back as each of the Warriors hopped down from the secret room. "You will notice," she said with businesslike efficiency, "that there are several latches up there. Should the authorities come looking for you, go up there, latch the trapdoor down securely, and then wait until I knock with the hatrack as follows." Taking the hatrack firmly, she rapped it upward three times, then twice, then three more times. She turned and said, "Understand?"

"I think that is well within our intellectual parameters," said Parcival. He checked his wrist unit and frowned. He tapped it several times and, when he received no response, said, "Bhodi Li, help me off with this equipment."

Bhodi stepped behind Parcival and aided Parcival in removing the computer equipment on his back. He was astounded at the weight of it. Even with his Photon strength it was heavy, and he wondered just how strong "little" Parcival was anyway.

The rig was laid out on the ground and Parcival knelt down next to it to examine it. His bespectacled face was impassive, but Bhodi Li could tell that it was all the youngest Warrior could do to contain his grief. Parcival had no family to speak of, and his computer helped to eliminate some of the loneliness he must certainly feel.

He ran tentative fingers over the gaping hole, studied the mangled circuitry. He shook his head. "Hopeless," he pronounced. "Utterly hopeless."

The woman took a tentative step forward. "What . . . is that?" she asked.

Parcival didn't look up. "It's my—"

"Radio," Bhodi Li jumped in quickly. "That's a radio. Parcival likes to listen to music."

"He carries such a big thing with him all the time?"

"Well—" He remembered something his granddad had said. "This is the Big Band era, right? So he needs a big radio."

"Oh no, the radio looks small," she said, which puzzled Bhodi until he realized that little portable radios were something this woman had never seen.

Parcival, oblivious to the entire discussion, was shaking his head. "It's a dead weight. We won't be able to access it for any information at all."

"Can't you fix it?" asked Tivia.

Parcival raised his glasses and rubbed the bridge of his nose. "You don't understand, Tivia. The components I need for repairs simply don't exist. I'm good—the best there is," he said with a touch of pride, "but even I can't pull something from nothing. The microcircuitry I require are not to be had in . . ." He paused. "Just when are we?" he asked.

The woman shook her head. "You mean where are you, don't you? You're in Berlin. Germany," she added.

Bhodi stepped towards her and took one hand gently. He heard Tivia give that little huff of hers and he grinned to himself. "Actually, he did mean 'when.' We've been traveling for quite some time. We've kind of lost track of dates. What's the date?"

"June 2," she said.

"Year?"

She tilted her head again, and this time there was quiet amusement in her eyes. "Just how long have you been traveling?"

"The year," Tivia said from across the room.

The woman glanced at Tivia and looked back at Bhodi Li. "She is an impatient one. The year is 1944." She paused and then added, "A.D."

She laughed softly then, a disconcerting sound for the extremely serious-minded Photon Warriors to hear. Bhodi Li looked at her closely for the first time.

She was a short woman, not much over five feet tall. Her figure was slim, and she was wearing a simple black dress that fell below her knees. She wore little makeup, and her coal black hair was tied up in a severe bun. Her face was narrow, her chin pointed. Her eyes were almost as dark as her hair, and were quite large. She seemed young to Bhodi, but her face was already lined with concerns beyond her years.

Bhodi was astounded. Here he routinely fought against the hordes of the Warlord of Arr for huge stakes—the fate, although it sounded pretentious, of the universe. Yet compared to the odds this woman battled, he felt he might have the easier fight. "What's your name?"

"Gretta," she said. "Gretta Meuller."

He bowed smartly from the waist. "Gretta Meuller, we thank you for your hospitality, and for undertaking the risk of allowing us into your home. I am Bhodi Li."

She blinked in surprise and, after several tries, managed to repeat the strange combination of syllables. Bhodi indicated his companions. "The young fellow is Parcival, and the girl—sorry, woman," he amended at her furious look, "is Tivia. She's a princess," he told her in a confidential tone.

She looked at the three of them. "Well," she said finally, "you are certainly the oddest trio of American spies I have ever seen. I'm not quite certain who you intended to hide from, dressed in the odd way you are. Fortunately for you I'm prepared for guests. I have clothes you can change into.''

Tivia looked at Gretta suspiciously. "I am not removing my armor," she said flatly. "To make yourself vulnerable to your enemies is the height of folly.''

Once again Bhodi Li felt reluctantly compelled to agree with Tivia. "I think we'll keep our stuff on," he told Gretta, "just in case we have to make a quick exit.''

Gretta shrugged. "As you wish, although I wouldn't suggest you go out looking like that." She dropped her voice to a whisper. "You might attract attention.''

"You're probably right," said Bhodi Li.

"Well, come downstairs when you are ready. I'll have some schnapps ready for you and we'll discuss just where you are, who my connections are, and how we can manage to get you out of Germany—presuming that is your goal, of course." She turned and walked out the door, and they heard the clik-clak of her heeled shoes on the stairs.

"Boy, she's really sweet," said Bhodi Li. "I wonder where her folks are.''

"They probably died of sugar poisoning.''

Bhodi allowed Tivia's snide comment to pass. "June 2, 1944. Brother—something big happened in June of '44, but darned if I can remember what or where. Ring any bells with you, Parcival?''

He shook his head. "Computers have always been my strength. I was always lousy in history.''

"Well, it's not history any more," said Tivia brusquely. "It's the here and now, and the sooner you start getting used to that, the better we will all survive.''

"The best way we can survive," replied Bhodi Li, "is to find the Warlord's henchmen from Arr and blow them back to the future.''

"Great plan," said Parcival. "Just one problem. Where are the Warriors, and what are they up to?''

5

Impatience

Even those who were most faithful to Adolf Hitler whispered the name of the Gestapo with respect and a healthy amount of fear.

The Gestapo were the secret police, and secret was not a term used lightly. If the Gestapo wanted you, they took you. No pretty warrants were required, you didn't have your rights read to you, and you didn't get one phone call. What happened to you once they had you was the real secret, because few people ever came back to tell about it. Those who did would usually admit that there was questioning about something or other. But the fear they felt during the questioning was so overwhelming that they usually didn't much want to discuss it at all. No matter how innocent you were, the Gestapo had a knack for making you feel guilty.

Colonel Schliss was one of those who excelled at making people feel guilty.

Seated behind his large, ornate and completely uncluttered desk, Schliss was examining a report that disturbed him greatly. It appeared that despite their best efforts, there still existed within Germany, and most particularly Berlin, pockets of resistance to the Fuehrer. In a way, the squat, mostly bald, evil-looking man was as happy as he was irritated. If the Gestapo was able to ruthlessly excise every trace of opposition to the Fuehrer, then there might not be any need for the Gestapo, since they existed to eliminate disloyalty. On the other hand, as long as there were still people who spoke against the Fuehrer, privately or publicly, and as long as there were still people who endeavored to smuggle Jews, Gypsies or any undesirables out of the country, then the Gestapo was not being one hundred percent effective.

A curious paradox. To be successful could mean to put oneself out of business. Well, he would not ponder it any further. Colonel Schliss was basically a soldier. He took orders from those above him and issued orders to those below him. And he maintained his own loyalty to Adolf Hitler. That was what was important.

Schliss's perfectly-tailored uniform was black, with some medals and similar decorations on his chest. His hat hung on a hook nearby, and his black leather boots, which at that moment were propped on his desk, were so polished that they practically glowed. His office was large, his desk so far from the door that anyone entering had to cover a great deal of ground in order to get to him. This was quite deliberate. He felt it gave him a psychological advantage, that anyone he dealt with received the impression that they were playing on his home ground. Schliss was not a tall man, but his chair was built up to give him added height behind his desk. Behind him on the wall was a framed portrait of Hitler, looking severely over his shoulder at anyone whom Schliss might be facing. The portrait indicated Hitler's tacit approval of anything he said or did. And if there was one thing for certain, it was that the Fuehrer was a most powerful ally to have, even in spirit.

There was a brisk knock at the door. Without looking up, Schliss swung his feet down and called, "Enter."

Schliss's aide, Hauptmann, entered, walking with quick
steps across the large, ornately paneled room. His heels
clicked against the wooden floor until he got to the plush
carpet that extended several feet beyond the edge of Schliss's
desk. There he waited, standing smartly at attention, until
such time that the colonel deigned to look at him. He
glanced covertly at the portrait on the wall and felt a
mixture of pride and apprehension.

Schliss kept Hauptmann waiting another thirty seconds
before looking up. When he did, a question on his face,
Hauptmann smartly brought up one hand in a salute and
said, "Heil Hitler."

"Heil Hitler," said Schliss wearily, tossing off a salute.
As much as he respected, admired and feared the Fuehrer,
that incessant greeting was getting on his nerves. "What is
it, Hauptmann?"

"We are attempting to interrogate the three prisoners
that were taken this morning, Herr Colonel."

"Prisoners? Which prisoners? There are so many."

"The three oddly garbed ones who appeared in the
courtyard of our headquarters this morning, claiming to be
Aryans."

Schliss recalled them instantly. There were gates and a
high wall around the perimeter of the headquarters, and yet
somehow three bizarrely dressed individuals had shown up
at their front door, bypassing their external security as if
they had actually just materialized right in the courtyard.

"Oddly garbed hardly seems a sufficient way of de-
scribing them, wouldn't you say?" observed Schliss. "One
looked like a comic opera pirate, complete with peg leg.
One was virtually a zombie with some sort of odd attach-
ments to his head. And the third," and he repressed a
shudder, "I have never seen a more insane costume in my
life. It made him look like some sort of monster."

"Yes, Herr Colonel," Hauptmann agreed.

"So? Is there a problem? Have we found out where they
came from? How is the interrogation going?"

"As you know, Herr Colonel, considering the circumstances, we have been quite—circumspect—in our questioning thus far. I regret to report that results have been less than satisfactory."

Schliss blew out air impatiently. "What you are saying is that thus far subtle methods of persuasion have been ineffective."

"Yes, mein Herr."

He slammed a fist down so abruptly that a small container of pencils on his desk jumped as if startled. "Then use stronger methods! Do I have to think of everything around here, Hauptmann?"

"No, mein Herr. Heil Hitler."

Schliss mumbled a reply. Hauptmann turned smartly on his heel and left again.

With a shake of his head borne of long suffering, Schliss muttered, "I am surrounded by incompetents."

Ten minutes later there was the sound of an explosion, and the entire building shook. Schliss immediately leaped to his feet, pulling his weapon from its holster. An allied attack! That was the only answer. They were being bombed, here in the heart of Berlin. The audacity of the allies knew no bounds.

There was another explosion that knocked Schliss off his feet the moment he reached the hallway. A bust of Hitler sat perched on a pedestal in a corner of the hall and the explosion sent it toppling. With a gasp of horror Schliss dove forward and snared the bust, cushioning the fall with his chest. He sighed in relief as he staggered to his feet, tucking the bust under one arm and holding his Walther PPK straight out in front of him.

He heard the sound of running feet, and from the far end of the corridor five storm troopers suddenly appeared, clearly falling back from a superior fighting force. Hauptmann was with them and was barking orders at the top of his panicked lungs.

"Fire!" he screamed, pointing down the hall at the

enemy Schliss still could not see. "Fire, in the name of the Fuehrer!"

The troopers didn't need any urging. They brought their rifles to bear and fired in unison. There was a roar like a freight train and then the wall directly behind them exploded, as a power blast crackled in the air over their heads. A gaping hole appeared just behind them, and debris rained down on them. The soldiers fell back towards where Schliss was standing, firing frantically behind them at the still unseen enemy.

Schliss forced himself to view the scene dispassionately. There was more than enough panic around him. Someone was going to have to keep his head screwed on properly.

Then the enemy appeared around the corner.

Until that moment Schliss had assumed that Destructarr was simply a normal man in an outlandish costume. But at that moment, as Destructarr stood there with smoke billowing from his arm cannon and his free hand wielding his power ball (a metal ball with spikes on a club), Schliss realized with dull horror that he was not facing a human opponent.

Experimentally he raised his Walther and fired from barely twenty feet away at Destructarr. The bullet bounced off the alien, and although Destructarr was heavily armored, Schliss had the sick feeling that the armor wasn't necessary.

Destructarr had been looking around in momentary confusion. Close-quarters combat was not his strong point. He was much better at taking out city blocks from a distance. But the bullets bouncing off his rock-hard skin served as something to focus on. He turned towards Schliss, saliva pouring from his great jaws. His breath peeled off some of the wallpaper.

He took one step towards Schliss and the entire corridor shook under his weight. The soldiers and Hauptmann, who had been standing between Destructarr and Schliss, sud-

denly bolted. Schliss, however, stood his ground, not due
to bravery at all. It was actually as if his feet had become
rooted to the spot.

Step after thunderous step Destructarr approached the
frozen Gestapo man until barely a foot separated them.

He slowly opened his huge maw, with his immense
pointed teeth that could have bitten Schliss's head off
effortlessly, and then a low horrible laugh issued from his
throat—a laugh that quickly turned into a full-throated
roar.

The roar mingled with Schliss's howl of terror.

"Enough, matey."

Destructarr stopped and slowly turned at the voice behind him. Schliss had been so distracted by what seemed
to be his imminent death that he hadn't even noticed the
other two strangers to Berlin who had appeared behind
Destructarr.

Destructarr's voice was low and ponderous. "He's mine,"
he rumbled.

"We be needing his help, Destructarr, old mate," said
Pirarr. He strode forward on his one good leg and one peg
leg. "We be needing him to take us to Hitler, because
that's what the Warlord wants."

Destructarr was not easily put off. "Mine to kill," he
said, his voice becoming louder in his irritation.

Mandarr came up behind him, his vacant eyes glittering
behind the mask that had been grafted to his face. "Now,
my large friend," he said silkily, "I understand your
blood lust. It's even commendable. But how would the
Warlord feel if he knew that you're ready to rend our main
contact here limb from limb. Hmmm?" At the last he
rested his chin on Destructarr's shoulder.

Destructarr paused to ponder this. Mandarr added softly,
in that distracted way he had, "You wouldn't want to
wind up like Warriarr, would you?"

During this time Destructarr had lifted Schliss clear off

his feet, but with the invoking of the Warlord, Destructarr released his grip. Schliss fell to the ground. His rump hurt from the fall. He was still holding his gun, and for a moment he toyed with the idea of blasting away.

Pirarr picked up on the unspoken thought. "I wouldn't be advising it, matey. Destructarr here would just as soon step on your head as not. He's in a mean mood, and mean is as good as he gets."

Schliss's lips formed the question before he was actually able to get the words out. He forced the paralytic fear from his vocal cords and said, "What do you want?"

Pirarr came up on the other side of Destructarr and leaned on the malevolent alien with studied nonchalance. "Fairly simple really. We want to speak with your boss."

His eyes widened. "You wish to speak to the head of the Gestapo?"

Mandarr suddenly dropped down to Schliss's eye level. "We don't care about your piddling little club. We want Hitler."

"You're . . . you're mad," Schliss managed to get out.

"No," said Pirarr reasonably. "Annoyed, perhaps, that we have patiently spent the majority of the day in holding facilities. Annoyed that, instead of being treated as foreign dignitaries as we should be, we're made to feel like prisoners. Annoyed that some fool was just now trying to remove Destructarr's hide as if it were some sort of costume."

"Did they?" asked Schliss absently, trying to ignore the fact that he had given that order to have Destructarr's "costume" removed.

"They did. Now, matey," said Pirarr, and he waved his cutlass in random patterns. "You have a choice. Either you can be bringing us straight to this Hitler fellow. Or we can level this place and start over again. And perhaps the next people we go to for help will be a little less stubborn and will be allowed to keep their building." Slowly Pirarr made a casual gesture and Destructarr lifted up his arm laser cannon.

"Well?" asked Pirarr.

Schliss pondered the situation a moment, reviewed his options. Then he nodded and said, "Very well, I have a telephone in my office. Come with me."

Mandarr grinned from Destructarr's side. "The man has more sense than I would have credited him for."

6

Reflections in a Photon Eye

Bhodi Li slowly awoke on the thin mattress that lay on the floor upstairs. He half turned and moaned, his body aching from the uncomfortable position. Lying back down he looked about and saw the two mattresses that had held his companions were empty. Parcival and Tivia had gotten up and around early.

He blinked. The fine mesh of Tivia's costume lay on her mattress and pieces of her armor padding lay next to it. Bhodi raised an eyebrow.

He staggered to his feet. There was a single window and through it came a single beam of sunlight. Bhodi walked over to it, trying to get a glimpse of the city outside and, as he approached it, he was surprised to feel new strength coursing through his body. It was as if he derived strength from the light of the sun. He stretched again and this time felt power in his arms and legs, and he effortlessly leaped up to the window, which was a good five feet above his head. He hung from the windowsill for a moment, looking out over the city. There seemed to be something missing. Then with amusement he realized what it was. TV aerials.

He felt the sun on his face and murmured, "The light shines." Then he dropped to the ground and walked out of the small room, down the narrow steps to the next floor.

He passed a small room and the door opened. Tivia stepped out and Bhodi Li stopped dead in his tracks.

She was wearing a blue cloth robe. Her bare feet padded softly on the carpet.

It was odd. Bhodi Li (as Christopher Jarvis) had been to the beach many a time, and seen girls in the skimpiest of bikinis. Yet, since he had met Tivia, he had found that those little scraps of cloth, and what they covered, were far less intriguing than the lower half of Tivia's face. Always he had only seen Tivia's large brown eyes staring over the mesh that covered her from the bridge of her nose down.

He was destined to be curious still, for when Tivia came out of the bathroom, she had a towel wrapped around her head and face, Arab-style. Again her eyes peered out at him. Bhodi smirked. "I thought you never removed your armor, Tivia."

She glanced heavenward. "I do believe in cleanliness, Bhodi Li. And Gretta was kind enough to launder my attire while I bathed." She placed a hand provocatively on her hips. "You're a Photon Warrior now. Try to think like one instead of like a human schoolboy." She huffed, "Men," and walked down the hallway.

Gretta approached Bhodi. She was carrying a bundle of clothes under her arm. "Awake, are we? Just in case you're wondering, welcome to June 3, 1944." She smiled, and Bhodi Li couldn't help but notice that she had a gorgeous smile. She handed him the clothes. Bhodi felt the material—it seemed far different from the T-shirts and jeans to which he had become accustomed. "Shower and change," she instructed briskly. "I'll have your precious armor clean for you in the meantime. Just leave your,'' she glanced again at the bizarre (by her standards) clothing that Bhodi wore, ''things outside the door of the bathroom.''

Half an hour later Bhodi Li trotted down the stairs to the living room, feeling a lot more like Christopher Jarvis in the simple clothes he now wore. Tivia, back in her usual clothes, sat next to Parcival.

Parcival, who was also in his normal Photon outfit, his Cleveland Indians baseball cap pushed up back on his head, sat hunched over his computer. His face had become the impassive mask that it always was when he was deep in concentration. He sat in front of a large, chest-high cabinet, which Bhodi Li suddenly recognized to be an old-style radio. Parcival had gutted the front of it and there were now hundreds of pieces of tubing and wire spread all over the living room floor.

Without looking up, Parcival said, ''Watch your left foot, Bhodi.'' Bhodi glanced down and saw that he had been about to step on some assorted radio parts.

''Sorry,'' he said and gingerly stepped around it. ''How's it going, Parcival? Decided to take a stab at fixing your gear after all?''

He nodded. ''We have nothing to lose by trying. MOM gave us valuable information that we'll need access to.''

Bhodi stepped as close as he could to Parcival without crunching something, knelt down next to the absorbed computer wizard and said, ''Parcival . . . are you at all concerned about MOM?''

Both Parcival and Tivia looked up at him with an expression that Bhodi had seen before—in the eyes of kids who had just been told that there is no Santa Claus. ''What in the world are you talking about, Bhodi?''

''Well, like . . .'' Bhodi cleared his throat. ''Well, for example, I'm speaking German whenever I speak to Gretta. How am I managing that?''

''Obviously, Bhodi, because of the translation device in your ear,'' said Parcival, looking at Bhodi Li oddly. ''In addition to providing translation, it also schools you in the language so that you can speak it. Otherwise it wouldn't be much of a translation device, would it?''

Parcival made it sound so reasonable. "But why didn't MOM tell us that?'' asked Bhodi.

Tivia laughed, although it was hardly a laugh of amusement. "Are you saying that just because MOM didn't spell out everything for us, there's something wrong with her?''

"No, it's just that—aw, never mind. You're probably right. Parcival, how long do you think it'll take?''

"I don't know," Parcival shrugged. "It'll take as long as it takes. In the meantime, why don't you talk with Gretta and see if you can figure out where the Dark Guardians might be right now.''

"Absolutely," agreed Tivia. "The sooner we find them, the sooner we can accomplish our mission and be back to our own time.''

Bhodi nodded and, still taking care not to step on anything Parcival might need, made his way to the kitchen. He heard eggs crackling on a skillet and grinned. It almost made it feel like home again.

He entered the kitchen, marveling at the old-style stove and refrigerator, and had to remind himself once again that it wasn't as if everything was outdated. The only thing out of its era was him.

Gretta was busy scrambling the eggs in the skillet, but she gave Bhodi a quick smile. "Your friends have already eaten. You're the last one this morning.''

"Yeah," said Bhodi, taking a seat at the small kitchen table. "I get comments like that a lot. What time is it?''

"A little after nine in the morning. From what your friends were discussing with each other, you have a fairly busy day ahead of you." She paused. "At least, from what I have managed to overhear. Every time they see me nearby, they become quiet very quickly.''

Bhodi started to say something but closed his mouth again. Gretta took the skillet and slid the eggs onto a plate.

As she did, Bhodi took the time to study her. It was odd—he had a hard time figuring out just how old she was. She seemed to have such a young face that it was difficult for Bhodi to conceive just what she had been through to make her look so careworn. She wore an apron over her simple white blouse and skirt. As she handed him the plate with the eggs on it, he thought about the day before, when they had been seated in her living room and she had filled them in on just what the setup was.

"I work with the Allied underground, as you might suspect from what you've seen," she had said. Bhodi had been able to tell that she was trying not to stare at their outlandish costumes. "This is a safe house—as safe, I should say, as any place is in Berlin. I give refuge to people who are fleeing from the authorities."

"You mean criminals?" asked Tivia warily.

"Oh, dear girl, criminals by the definitions of the Gestapo perhaps. If being born the 'wrong' race is what makes you a criminal."

"But that's absurd," said Tivia. "You're not born a criminal. It's your deeds, not your background, that marks you as an evil person."

"Not here," was the bitter reply. "Here you are taken away for being the wrong religion, the wrong color—even being in the wrong place at the wrong time." With an effort she erased the sorrow from her voice and went back to business. "People hide out here until we manage to smuggle them out. It is a dangerous game we play here."

"Sounds like the only game in town," said Bhodi.

Gretta nodded. "I will be in touch with my contacts in the underground. How I will be in touch with them need not concern you. I sense that getting out of Berlin is not your greatest priority."

"We'll get out when we're ready to get out," said Bhodi. He removed his helmet and put it on the table next to him. "What we need you to find out for us is information. We're looking for three . . . I don't think you could call them people exactly. Most certainly at least one of them looks like an out-and-out monster. Another looks like a green-skinned, one-eyed pirate. And the third looks like the Lone Ranger on acid.''

Gretta stared at him. "Like who on what?"

"He, uhm, he has kind of a mask." Bhodi made circles of his fingers and put them around his eyes. "And he talks and acts pretty weird. They're the ones we're after. If you can tell your people to be on the lookout for them, we'll be set."

That had been yesterday.

Today, as Bhodi hungrily started to devour the eggs, Gretta leaned forward and said, "Thus far I haven't heard anything through my connections about the three you seek. But as soon as I do, you'll be the first to know."

"Well, we can't wait around," said Bhodi, eggs filling his mouth. "We're going to have to scout around."

"How are you going to do that?"

"You must have some coats or something around here. We'll toss on the coats and just walk around. No one should notice us as long as they don't see our weapons."

Gretta frowned and said, "I'm not certain how to tell you this, but I can't recall seeing people with the skin coloring of your friends all that frequently—certainly not since the Fuehrer came into power and people started . . . disappearing. They are quite certain to attract attention."

Bhodi started in surprise. Ever since he had "found the light," as MOM called it, he had fought side by side with Parcival and Tivia and never once had skin color ever been a consideration in their struggles. He had never really thought of Parcival as a ten-year-old black kid, which he was, nor had the dark hues of Tivia's skin really penetrated.

"You're right," he murmured. "MOM should have thought of that."

"Your mother should have known?"

"No, not . . ." He smiled. "Forget it. And I think I'll forget it, too. If I imply to Parcival and Tivia that MOM made a mistake, they'll just give me grief again." He was silent for a moment, and then he said, "Where's your mom? And dad? Do they live in Berlin, too?"

Gretta, who had appeared just moments before to look about twenty-five, now allowed lines to appear in her face that made her look forty. "They're dead," she said tonelessly.

"I'm sorry."

"So am I," she said. "They were killed during Crystal Night."

He blinked. "What's Crystal Night?"

"There was a massive display against German Jews," she said, trying to keep her voice neutral. "Massive destruction of private property. Windows broken, buildings defaced and damaged while rioting and looting went on. Our neighbors, who were Jews, were assaulted, and my parents went out to try and help them." She paused. "My parents were killed in the melee." She shook her head. "So many Gentiles tried to ignore what was happening to our Jewish neighbors. My parents, they tried to set an example of showing how we can't close our eyes to violence and injustice, and they paid for it. That's why I swore to continue their work. But quietly, in a more covert manner, so that I could accomplish more. I'm trying to be true to their memories."

"And the Jews?" asked Bhodi. "What has been happening to them?"

"They were 'relocated'—the term the authorities used." She smiled a mirthless smile. "That's correct, I suppose. They were taken off to camps and have probably been exterminated by this time. Relocated from this life to the next."

Bhodi was horrified. "They just . . . just took German citizens off and killed them?" His jaw was set and he reached for his Photon Phaser automatically before he realized that he wasn't wearing it. "Where are these camps? Let's go get them out."

She shook her head. "That's not possible. Not even for you and your remarkable friends. You must concentrate on your small battles, Bhodi Li, and allow the fates to attend to the Nazis and their ilk."

Bhodi, who had been half out of his chair, slowly sat back down. He stared at the remaining eggs and realized that he had lost his appetite. He pushed the plate away and shrugged apologetically.

"Bhodi Li," said Gretta, stumbling a little as always over his unusual name, "where are your parents?"

Bhodi made no reply, and Gretta pushed gently. "The weaponry of your friends and yourself, your way of talking, your entire mission—Bhodi, what is going on? Just exactly who have I given sanctuary to? I'd very much like to know."

Bhodi sat back, tilting on the back legs of his chair. It was true. They had taken refuge in this woman's home, involved her however tangentially in their battle. In short they were trusting her with their very lives, and yet they hadn't trusted her enough to tell her what the real score was.

"My parents," he said slowly, "haven't been born yet."

She tilted her head in that way she had. "Now, that wasn't an answer I was expecting."

"I'm not surprised. Me, and Parcival and Tivia—we're all Photon Warriors. Photon is," he paused, trying to think of the best way to phrase it, "Photon is a life energy in the form of a crystal sphere. It represents light and hope. It's—"

"It's what's missing in much of Europe these days," said Gretta ruefully.

"You got that right," said Bhodi. "Any planet in the universe is arid and lifeless until exposed to Photon energy. If a Photon Warrior, such as myself, activates the Photon energy, the planet is filled with green, growing life. But there are dark forces, headed by a . . . being, I suppose . . . called the Warlord of Arr, who wants to try and use the Photon energy for evil. If one of his Dark Guardians activates a Photon crystal, the planet becomes dark and evil, like the Warlord himself. The three guys we're after are Dark Guardians.''

''And these Dark Guardians . . . they want to activate a crystal on this planet?'' Her tone was noncommittal.

''No. They're here to recruit Adolf Hitler for their cause. Now, in my time—over forty years from now—Hitler was defeated. But the Dark Guardians could screw all that up. If they do, they could wind up changing time completely. And if that happens, then my entire world will be different, and I might not even be born.''

There was long silence, and then Gretta took Bhodi's chin affectionately in her hand. ''All right, Bhodi,'' she said. ''Don't tell me who you are. But you don't have to make up stories.''

Bhodi's mouth dropped open. She was just like his grandfather! ''Brother, sometimes it just doesn't pay to tell the truth.'' He leaned forward. ''You want to hear about how I was recruited? How I got over 2,500 points at the Photon Center, and MOM the super-computer, and the first Guardian of Photon, transported me up to Intellistar to be a Photon Warrior? I could tell you about Pike or Leon or Lord Baethan. Or—''

She waved him off as she started to wash the skillet in the big sink. ''Bhodi, you are so imaginative. And I appreciate what you did.''

''Wh-what'd I do?''

''You saw how sad I was, thinking about my parents, and you wanted to do something to cheer me up. So you launched into that entire preposterous story to take my mind off my problems. Well, it worked.'' She walked over to him and kissed him lightly on the forehead. ''Thank you.''

Bhodi sat there and then shrugged. ''You're welcome.''

7

Doing the Town

It had started to rain.

Bhodi stared out the window and a slow smile spread. He was back in his Photon rig and itchy for action. But since none was immediately forthcoming, he decided to try and make some.

He walked into the sitting room. Tivia was seated at a table with an array of playing cards in front of her, shaking her head. Gretta stood behind her patiently, saying, "See? Now you can put red four on black five."

Tivia shook her head. "This is a waste," she said. "What is gained by playing pointless games like this solitaire when I could be practicing my fighting skills? A princess of Nivia has to have her priorities."

Gretta patted her on the shoulder. "Everyone needs mindless recreation every now and then. Besides, these days any distraction from what is going on around us is to be welcomed."

"Tivia," Bhodi said, "let's get out for a while. Walk around and keep a low profile. Maybe we'll get lucky and spot the Dark Guardians."

Tivia glanced at him. "The idea has merit," she admitted. "It beats sitting around waiting for Parcival to fix his computer. But we will have to be cautious."

"Hey, sure. My middle name is cautious," he said cheerfully. Tivia merely snorted.

Within minutes they had donned heavy coats and hats to protect them against the heavy rains that had begun. In addition Tivia wrapped a scarf around the lower half of her face to cover the mesh. Bhodi snickered. Tivia, who made such a big deal about being against men, looked like a man in the heavy coat. The padding of her armor gave her additional bulk. She snapped, "What are you smirking at?"

"Smirking, Princess? I'm not smirking," said Bhodi, smirking.

Together they stepped through the front door, glanced left and right. There were no soldiers, at least not in evidence. Bhodi felt creeping paranoia—who knew where men from the Gestapo might be hiding? It was something. He had only been here such a short time and already he felt like eyes were watching his every move. How must it be for those who were really a part of this time?

They walked out into the streets of Berlin.

The clouds had completely covered any trace of the sun. It might as well have been night. Bhodi and Tivia, buoyed by the Photon strength in their bodies, were little affected by the driving wind that wanted to shove them back.

Bhodi looked around him as he walked. In school he had seen films about World War II. Because of the age of the newsreels, everything he had ever seen had such an unnatural air to it. It had been difficult to even think of it as real.

But it was real now. Watching people buffeted by the wind and alternately joking with one another or just silently struggling, Bhodi felt the unreality that the past had always had for him wash away. These were people, humans, just as human as himself. Facts about the war that had been just words on paper started to take on a new meaning to him.

Tivia tapped him lightly on the shoulder. "You look like you're daydreaming. Snap out of it."

"Sorry," he muttered.

Abruptly there was a loud honking behind them and Bhodi realized that they had been walking in the street. Not a sharp move. Automatically Bhodi started to leap, but Tivia held him firmly by the arm and they ran to the sidewalk. Bhodi realized immediately why she had done it—it wouldn't have been the most brilliant maneuver to let people see them vault ten feet. He gave her a quick, appreciative glance and she nodded.

The transport truck drove by, splashing up water on Bhodi and Tivia. Bhodi looked at the back of the truck, expecting to see more of the soldiers they had fought the day before.

He saw soldiers, all right. And something else. Just as the truck rounded a corner, Mandarr glanced out the back.

Bhodi staggered, as if punched. "Tivia! Did you—"

"Yes, I did. Let's go," was the terse reply.

This time they tossed aside caution and started to bound after the truck, their Photon-energized leaps eating up the distance between themselves and the speeding truck. They rounded the corner and saw the truck turning another corner. Bhodi pulled his Phaser from beneath the folds of his coat. "I'm going to take out the truck," he said.

"Can you do it without blowing it up?" demanded Tivia. "Killing an entire squad of soldiers wouldn't do much for keeping the time stream on track."

Bhodi cursed silently and then said, "Come on."

They kept on running, as fast as they could. They were just going around another corner when they ran into the one thing they could have done without.

More soldiers. On foot. And Bhodi, not having the time to reverse his charge, smacked right into them.

. . .

Parcival bent intensely over the pieces scattered all over the floor. His lips pursed, he didn't hear Gretta's first three offers of hot cocoa, and she finally gave up.

Even as he worked, he wondered about his own family. Were his parents born yet? Where were his grandparents? He had never known either, having grown up for as long as he could remember in the orphanage.

They had made fun of him in the orphanage, the runty little kid who couldn't keep up in football or soccer, who admired baseball so much that he was never seen without the cap of his favorite baseball team—yet when a game was being organized, he was never chosen until the last.

Parcival the runt. Parcival the four-eyes.

Until he had discovered the Photon centers, and then he was Parcival, the Photon Warrior. And once he had been recruited by MOM, his life had turned around. He had joined the Photon Guardians and had never looked back.

It was odd for Parcival. This had been his first trip back to Earth in over a year, for he lived full-time on Intellistar. He had wondered whether, if he ever went back, Earth would be the way he remembered it. Whether things would be different. Boy, he never could have imagined j#how different it would be.

Even as all this went through his mind, his skilled hands automatically went through the motions of repairing his beloved computer.

He sat up, his back starting to ache for the first time after his hours of leaning over. He smiled and shook his head in wonderment. "Parcival, my man, you're a bigger genius than they give you credit for." He patted the computer, which was now hooked up to hundreds of little bits of wire and tubing cannibalized from the radio Gretta had graciously given him.

He picked up his wrist console, his main means of accessing the computer. He pressed several buttons, keying in the code name that would put him on-line.

Nothing happened.

He frowned. There was nothing wrong with the wrist unit, he was certain of that. And his repairs on his computer back-pack, although jury-rigged, should have worked. He sat on his haunches, trying to figure out where he had gone wrong.

"Parcival?"

He turned at her voice. "Yes?"

"Ah, so you're talking to me now," said Gretta with a smile. At his look of confusion, she said softly, "Never mind. How are your repairs on your . . . radio . . . coming?"

He sighed. "It should be working. It's not. I've done everything right, I'm sure."

"Maybe I could help. I'm somewhat handy."

Parcival coughed politely. "I don't think so. I'm sure that my endeavors are somewhat beyond your current"—he wanted to say technology—"expertise," he finished.

"Oh." She was silent for a moment. "You're sure you've done everything right. It should work?"

"Yes, it should," he said with a touch of impatience.

"Is it plugged in?"

"Of course it's . . . it's . . ." His voice trailed off.

He flipped the pack over and ran his fingers over the energy module on the side. He grinned sheepishly. He had been so concerned about fixing the actual circuitry he had clean forgotten to check the power source, which had also been damaged by the bullets. "No. It's not plugged in." He shook his head. "I owe you an apology, Gretta. You're quite right. But with the energy module on the fritz, I have no way of powering this up."

"Could you plug it into a normal outlet? I have an extra cord around."

Parcival shrugged and a bit of his usual confidence began to return. "If anyone can, I can. Let's give it a shot."

The rain seemed to come down heavier as Bhodi and Tivia faced the two dozen soldiers in front of them. Bhodi rapidly shoved his Phaser into the large pocket of his coat.

"I'm sorry," he said quickly to the man in the lead. "Please pardon my clumsiness." He began to despair as the truck disappeared in the distance.

The soldier nodded curtly. "You should be more careful."

"Yes, I know. Sorry." Bhodi and Tivia started to back up so that they could walk around the soldiers.

At that moment a huge gust of wind came up. It blew off Bhodi's hat, which was not that much of a problem, particularly since he had the good sense to have left his helmet back in the house.

It also blew off Tivia's hat, and this *was* a problem. The upper half of her face and her full black hair was now fully exposed.

The lead soldier, who had been so polite a moment ago, immediately took a surprised step backward. "Who is this Negress?" he demanded.

"What's a Negress?" said Tivia in a low voice.

"I'll tell you later," Bhodi shot back. Then he said quickly, "She's my cousin. Skin condition. You understand."

His curiosity thoroughly aroused, the soldier reached for the scarf that covered the lower half of her face.

Her reflex was automatic from a lifetime of being taught to keep men at arm's length. Tivia grabbed his forearm, dragged him forward and sent a side snapkick into the pit of his stomach. She then turned, using her back as a fulcrum, and in one smooth motion sent the soldier flying over her left shoulder.

That tore it, thought Bhodi Li, and even as the thought crossed his mind his Photon Phaser was in his hand. The soldiers were stunned for only a moment, and before they had their rifles unslung from their shoulders, Bhodi had his Phaser pointed at the head of the fallen trooper.

"One move and he gets it!" called out Bhodi.

As one the soldiers all swung their rifles around and aimed them point-blank at Bhodi and Tivia.

Good bluff, thought Bhodi. Should've worked.

Tivia looked around desperately and spotted, several stories up, a small balcony overlooking the street. With all their eyes on Bhodi, none of the soldiers noticed as Tivia yanked out her own Phaser and fired upward.

The Phaser beam sliced through the supports of the balcony in a split second, and with a screech of metal and stone the balcony started to fall to the street.

"Scatter!" shouted one of the troopers, and they dashed helter-skelter to avoid the falling debris.

Bhodi grabbed Tivia by the arm. "Let's get out of here!" he shouted.

Tivia broke into a run next to him, but he heard her murmur, "I hate running from stupid men."

Within seconds they had rounded the corner, but then they heard the sounds of running feet behind them. A shot whizzed past Bhodi's ear. Instinctively he turned to fire back but stopped himself. His Phaser beam would cut the soldiers in half, no two ways about that. And he couldn't kill them. He just couldn't.

He and Tivia started covering distance in huge leaps, gaining ground. Rain poured across their faces, making it hard to see, although if it was hard for them to see, then it would be hard for the soldiers to see as well.

Suddenly Tivia went down with a yell. For one horrible moment Bhodi thought that she had been hit. But she was already staggering to her feet. There had been a pothole in the street, a deep one that had filled up with rainwater, and Tivia had landed one foot right in it. It had caught her by surprise, and now when she took a step forward she moaned, staggering.

Oh boy, she twisted her ankle, thought Bhodi, and there was no time to be delicate. With a hasty "Sorry about this, Tivia," he grabbed her around the waist and slung her under his arm.

"Hey!" she shouted, but Bhodi was already leaping, her weight slowing him down only a little.

Shots were fired again, and Bhodi felt one bounce off

the armor under his coat. That was a relief, but if they hit
his head—well, Tivia had called him thick-headed, but
his skull was scarcely armor-plated.

At that moment, soldiers came down the other end of
the street. Didn't anyone know enough to stay in out of the
rain on a day like this? Bhodi wished he had known
enough.

Responding to shouts of "Halt!" from the pursuing
soldiers, the new arrivals immediately started towards Bhodi
and Tivia. They darted down another side street, the soldiers giving chase.

Tivia had stopped pounding on his chest and was now
holding on for dear life. Bhodi, for his part, was beginning
to get out of breath, even with his superior strength. His
breathing was getting ragged, and he felt weighted down
both by Tivia and by the rain-soaked clothing.

He turned and, in hopes of throwing them off, ran down
an alley.

Dead end.

He realized it only when he was halfway down. He
spun, but the exit from the alley was cut off by soldiers
now crowding around it. Bhodi backed up as far as he
could before he bumped against the wall. He was surrounded on all three sides by buildings too high even for
him to jump. There were windows overhead on all sides,
and light from within the buildings was the only illumina-
tion in the darkened alley. But it was enough for the
soldiers to see them by.

"I think we've got a problem," said Tivia drily. "Care
to put me down so I can die on my feet?"

Bhodi set her on the ground. She balanced gingerly,
favoring the injured ankle. Side by side they faced the
soldiers, both of them with their Phasers at the ready but
not sure how or if they should use them.

From the dimness next to him Bhodi heard Tivia say,
"Bhodi Li, I just want you to know—all those insulting
things I've said about you in the past . . .?"

"Yeah?"

She chucked him on the shoulder. "Nothing personal."

"Gee, thanks."

Several blocks away Parcival stared apprehensively at the plug in his hand and the wall socket into which he was about to insert it. He shook his head. "I've got a bad feeling about this."

Gretta looked from the plug to Parcival and back again. "Do you have any other options?"

"Nope."

He took a deep breath and inserted the plug.

He paused for a moment, holding his breath. He looked over at his computer and immediately it lit up. Even though it was silent, he could practically feel his equipment surging to electronic life.

"All right!" he breathed. "It worked."

Gretta wrinkled her nose. "Something's burning."

"Oh no!"

Parcival leaped away a second before sparks started pouring out of the wall socket and, simultaneously, out of his computer. Parcival tried to grab the cord to yank it out of the wall, but when he touched it, he pulled his hand back. It tingled from the electrical shock it had received.

"It needs too much power!" shouted Parcival over the crackling sounds that filled the room. "We've got to shut down before— "

Every light in the house blew out at once and they were plunged into darkness.

"It's just the fuses," shouted Gretta. "Don't get so frantic."

Parcival, working by touch in the dark, frantically punched in codes to his wrist unit. "You don't understand," he said tersely. "It'll keep draining energy from wherever it can until it's fully powered. It might black out Europe before it's through . . . there!" The hum that filled the room abruptly stopped.

Parcival ran to the window, banging his shin on the coffee table. He looked out and saw exactly what he thought he would. The entire section of the city had been blacked out.

"Oh boy," muttered Parcival. "Bhodi and Tivia are going to be really steamed."

The alleyway suddenly became pitch-black.

The leader of the squadron of soldiers squinted, no longer able to make out his quarry. Not yet realizing that the entire city had gone black thanks to Parcival's massive power surge, he decided that his men were now at a disadvantage. He took no chances.

"Fire at will!" he shouted.

There was a smashing of glass from down in the alley but they ignored it. They opened fire.

The soldiers began filling the alleyway with flying lead. Tivia and Bhodi Li were many things, but bulletproof they were not. The bullets spelled a quick and violent death for the Photon Warriors.

That is, of course, had they been there.

At the moment the lights went, Bhodi and Tivia seized their chance. Grabbing each other's hands they leaped straight up towards one of the windows in the building to their right. It was closed, and they smashed through it just as bullets started cutting through the air beneath them.

They were in a small apartment that was apparently empty. Barely slowing down Bhodi and Tivia bolted through it and out the front door, leading into a narrow corridor. Tivia glanced around and Bhodi spotted some stairs leading upward. "C'mon!" he hissed and without waiting to see if she followed, went up the stairs two at a time.

He kept going up and then smashed through a final door that led out onto the roof. Tivia was at his side a moment later. They looked over the darkened city, and Bhodi let out a low whistle. "Somebody up there likes us," he said.

"You're right about that," said Tivia. "Which way now?"

"How do I know?"

"It's your planet, isn't it?" she said in exasperation.

Bhodi glanced over the edge of the roof and saw the troopers massing around the opening of the alley. "Well, not that way." He turned and pointed in the opposite direction. "That way. We'll take the high road."

They started to leap from one roof to the next. Down on the ground citizens came pouring out of their homes, heedless of the rain, asking each other what had happened. Was it an air raid? Could the allies be attacking?

Bhodi and Tivia didn't stick around to find out what the general consensus was. They hopped from roof to roof like oversized kangaroos, putting as much distance between themselves and the soldiers as they could. In the darkness no one spotted them, particularly with the heavy rain making it all but impossible to look up.

Bhodi glanced back to see that although Tivia was still favoring one leg slightly, she seemed to be handling herself just fine. He then turned back and leaped to the next roof on their route.

But he miscalculated. The roof was angled, not flat, and when he hit it, his boots slid right down the slick shingles. The treads on his soles did nothing to slow his skid and he fell straight down to the street.

"Bhodi!" Tivia shouted down. "Bhodi, say something! Are you okay?" No answer. "Bhodi!"

From the darkness below floated the response, "You care!"

Under her half mask Tivia's lips twitched in amusement, but her voice was deliberately stern. "Bhodi Li, if you get yourself killed, it could seriously hamper our mission. We need you, for cannon fodder, if nothing else."

Figuring if he could survive the drop, she certainly could, Tivia gracefully leaped off and landed in the dark-

ness of the alley. She landed on what felt like old mattresses, which cushioned her fall. She sat there for a
moment and surveyed the darkness around her. "Bhodi?"
she whispered.

The mattress moaned. She jumped up and Bhodi Li,
shakily, got to his feet. "You didn't have to land on me,"
he complained.

"Don't crab. It's unseemly for a Photon Guardian."

They didn't exchange many words as they made their
way back to Gretta's home. The rain was starting to slow
up, but it was too little too late. Tivia could see that Bhodi
was angry with himself over having seen Mandarr only to
let him get away. To her surprise almost as much as his,
Tivia said, "Bhodi, you did your best."

"I let him get away," said Bhodi. "If I'd been faster, I
could have gotten off a shot right at him. Blasted him right
back to the Warlord."

"You expect too much of yourself, Bhodi."

He turned to her. "No less than you expect of yourself."

"Well," she shrugged. "That's completely different.
After all, you're—"

"Only a man," he completed for her. "I've heard the
song before. Look, Princess, there's something I want to
tell you— "

But Tivia wasn't listening. She had stopped in front of
a door, which Bhodi had not immediately recognized as
Gretta's home. But then, he was only a man, he thought.

They stepped through the door, and Parcival immediately came up to them holding a candle. "I'm sorry," he
began.

"Sorry? Sorry for wh—" Then Bhodi caught on. "You
did this? You blacked out the city?"

"Yes. Apparently I made some miscalculations as to the
amount of energy my computer would require to operate.
The city should be up and running before long, however."

Bhodi, laughing, put a hand on Parcival's shoulder.
"Parcival, my friend, your computer saved our hash."

He looked from Bhodi to Tivia in confusion. "It did?"
Tivia nodded confirmation.

"Well, in that case, it worked out. I guess." It was
pleasing to Bhodi to see the normally "all-answers" Parcival
at a loss.

"It certainly did," said Tivia. "If it weren't for you, we
might be dead in this godforsaken era—no offense, Gretta.
Thanks to this fortuitous power drain of yours, we got
away completely."

"No one followed you?" asked Gretta in concern.

"Absotively, posilutely not," said Bhodi. "Not with
the route we followed—nobody short of Spider-Man could
have kept up with us."

There was a pounding at the door. "Open up! Gestapo!"

"How about that?" said Parcival. "Spider-Man's a member of the Gestapo."

8

Fuehrer Furor

"We are not accustomed to being kept waiting, little men," said Mandarr.

The two members of Hitler's personal bodyguard stood at attention outside the ornate double doors that led from the smaller outer office into the immense inner sanctum of Adolf Hitler. Mandarr, Pirarr and Destructarr were already not happy—being carted around in a truck was not the sort of transportation to which they had become accustomed. It was hardly the sleek journey that space travel gave one. The Nazis had pointed out that Destructarr would not fit into a standard vehicle, and that it would not have been wise to separate the hulking Dark Guardian from his fellows. Both of these were valid points, but that didn't mean that Mandarr had to like them.

Pirarr said in a low tone, "Mateys, don't you think you should be showing us in? Just in case Destructarr here starts to get hungry and wants a snack. Like you, for example."

They glanced blandly at Destructarr. "That absurd costume doesn't bother us," one of them said.

Mandarr seemed almost amused by this. "Is that a

fact? Oh, Destructarr . . ." He pointed towards a large, solid mahogany desk that weighed at least a couple of hundred pounds, and he made an arm-flexing movement. Destructarr nodded, strode over to the desk and lifted it. With absolutely no visible strain Destructarr raised the desk completely over his head.

Mandarr looked blandly at the two personal guards. "How would you like to have my little friend throw that desk right through the doors to your precious Fuehrer's office, hmmm?"

One of them blanched and the other, gulping visibly, gently rapped on the door without removing his gaze from Destructarr and the potential missile. "Mein Fuehrer," he said, and again, "Mein Fuehrer."

The doors were thrown wide open and Hitler, furious at the interruption, stood there.

Instantly Pirarr felt it and glanced at Mandarr. He felt it as well. Destructarr, being far more muscle than brain, didn't feel much of anything, but he didn't have to. It was there regardless. That same feeling of power and strength and pure, unrelenting evil that they felt whenever they stood before the Warlord of Arr.

Out of long habit Mandarr lowered his voice in deference. "Good day, mein Fuehrer." Then he put up a hand, palm facing Hitler, and said, "Heil you."

Hitler stared at them, wonderment growing in his eyes. There was a burning intensity in that little man's stare. His thin, black hair was plastered down on his head, and he had a small, narrow moustache. He looked from one of the Dark Guardians to the other, staring the longest at Mandarr, before he gestured quickly, "Come in. Come in."

They followed him into his office. There were a dozen bodyguards within the office, each staring at the three Dark Guardians with a mixture of fear and loathing. Only Hitler was completely unafraid. He stepped right up to Mandarr, staring deeply into his eyes. "Are you . . . from beyond?" he asked.

"From beyond this paltry world? Yes."

Hitler clenched his fists in excitement. "I knew it. As soon as the Gestapo told me about you—about what you were capable of—I knew you were from beyond. I have always believed strongly in the supernatural," and he stared at his guards, "although there are some who think me mad for doing so."

"I'm certainly not among them, matey," began Pirarr.

And Hitler turned on him, so swiftly that their minds had not even had time to register the change. "You shall not address me in that familiar manner! Is that clear?"

Taken aback by the intensity of this man, Pirarr dropped his gaze. "All right."

"You shall address me as mein Fuehrer or not at all! Is that understood?"

"Understood," said Pirarr with startling meekness.

The knuckles in his fist clenched and unclenched for a moment. Then in a brittle voice he said to Mandarr, "Rommel becomes more popular all the time. He is of value to me, but there should be no one whose voice is equal to mine."

Mandarr nodded. "That would be Field Marshal Rommel. The Desert Fox. He will live for a time longer, but eventually will be invited to commit suicide. He will accept the invitation," he finished with a small smile.

Hitler lifted an eyebrow. "You speak as if this has already occurred."

"To us, it already has. We are from your future, mein Fuehrer," said Mandarr silkily. "And I happen to be very familiar with this little war of yours. You see . . . before I came from . . . out there," and he inclined his head upward, "I came from your planet. I am an earthling . . ."

"Although we don't hold that against him," Pirarr said, and as an afterthought added, "mein Fuehrer." Hitler noticed and nodded in silent approval.

"Before I discovered the power of the Dark, I studied a great deal of history. Particularly war. I can tell you a great many things. I can help you win this war."

Hitler frowned. "I *will* win this war. It is preordained."

Slowly, Mandarr shook his head. "No. The allies win, and you kill yourself in your bunker."

With a shout of immeasurable fury Hitler yanked his pistol from his holster. He pointed it straight at Mandarr's face. "I could kill you for that!"

Mandarr stared down the business end of the Walther PPK. Then, incredibly, he smiled. "I wouldn't recommend that, mein Fuehrer."

"Why not?"

"Three reasons. First, my large friend Destructarr has that arm cannon of his aimed right at you."

Hitler glanced over and saw this was indeed the case. Destructarr was so massive that Hitler had not noticed the huge weapon on his arm or that it was now looking his way.

"Second," and suddenly Mandarr's Phaser was in his hand, "I'm from beyond, remember? We're very quick draws in the beyond. And third—if you do manage to get lucky and kill me, you condemn yourself to follow what history has laid out for you."

Hitler stared askance at him. "You're bluffing."

"Think so? Shall I tell you the date you die so you can have it to look forward to? All right. It's—"

"No!"

There was dead silence in the great office for a full minute. Hitler's eyes narrowed, and he was clearly calculating all the possibilities.

Finally he lowered his gun, and Mandarr slowly lowered his as well. Then the Fuehrer, the leader of the Third Reich, walked around to the other side of his desk and sat down. Behind him was a huge red flag draped on the wall, and on the flag was a giant swastika.

He leaned forward and said, "Let us talk."

9

Perspectives

Parcival slid the trapdoor into place with a tap of his foot and the Photon Warriors were once more within the darkness of the attic.

They were silent for a time, straining their ears to detect the slightest conversation from the first floor. But they could hear nothing.

"You think Gretta can handle them?" asked Parcival.

"I think Gretta can handle just about anything," replied Bhodi.

Bhodi could then feel Tivia's gaze upon him in the darkness. "You seem to admire this Gretta. I must admit I can understand why. She seems quite level-headed and aggressive. Are all Earth women this way?"

"Some. Some are together. Some are real airheads. Just like the men. We're all different."

There was a soft laugh but no humor in it. "Men are all the same. Oh, you and Parcival are exceptional for your gender, but overall . . ."

"Look, I don't want to hear this, Tivia, okay?" Bhodi leaned down and put his ear to the floor. It was frustrating.

He wanted to go down there, Phaser blasting, taking out whatever there might be threatening Gretta. But he knew he couldn't.

There was another silence and then Tivia said, "Bhodi Li?"

"What?"

"What is a Negress?"

He heard Parcival cough loudly. "It's . . . uhm . . . it's someone with dark skin. Really dark. Like yours and Parcival's."

"Is that a problem?"

He stood. "It was to the Nazis. My granddad told me that the Nazis locked away people who were . . . well, not the type they wanted. They'd put you away if you were the 'wrong' race, or religion, because the feeling was that those people were inferior."

The outrage in her voice was practically something you could touch. "They would think me inferior just because of the color of my skin?"

"Hey, don't sound so mad at me. That's not my philosophy."

"I know, but . . ." Her voice shook with fury. "So I did not imagine the derision in that man's tone of voice. Thank you for this firsthand history lesson into your planet's background, Bhodi Li. It's worse than I could have imagined."

"Oh yeah?" He turned on her then, his eyes starting to be able to make out her dim outline. "Don't get so snooty and highbrow with me, Tivia. You're not much better than the Nazis anyway."

Bhodi heard Parcival's shocked gasp before he heard Tivia say, "What are you talking about?" There was a dangerous edge to her voice.

Suddenly feeling that he would rather be wrestling with Dogarr about now than continuing this discussion, Bhodi nevertheless persisted. "I'm talking about how you're always carping that the women on your planet are so superior, and that men are all inferior. It's no different than the Nazis who said that all the Jews were inferior and all the Gypsies and other people. Oh sure, you don't slap all the men into concentration camps, like Grandpa said they did with people. But—''

"It's totally different," said Tivia.

"Sure, it always is. Everything's different when it's you yourself involved. Grandpa said that the German people let it all happen because they stuck their heads in the sand. The people who were taken away didn't think it would happen to them, and the people who were left didn't believe it was really happening. Everyone's real quick at denial and slow in taking responsibility. I understand that your whole planet doesn't have any men on it at all.''

"But that's—''

"Yeah, yeah. Different. Well, I don't think it's so different. You say men are inferior. The Nazis say you're inferior.''

"But they're wrong!'' she exploded. Parcival shushed her frantically.

"Exactly,'' said Bhodi Li. "And I just wish that you'd put aside your own stupid prejudices, 'cause, frankly, I think you're a better person than that, and you should be able to think for yourself. As long as you believe that all of anybody is inferior—be it men or any other group— then actually you'll be the one who's inferior.''

He waited then for the swift punch or kick that he thought would follow.

Instead there was a long silence. "Tivia—?''

"Do you really think I'm like them?'' came her quiet question.

"What do you care what I think?''

"I just do, all right? Answer my question. Is that what you think? That I'm like them?''

He reached out and placed a hand on her shoulder. He felt her automatically start to flinch away from him and then remain where she was. "No. Because I don't think they'd be able to rethink their philosophies. But you're smarter than they are, and you probably can.''

Parcival let out a long "phew" and realized that he'd been holding his breath.

"You make quite a persuasive argument, Bhodi Li."

"Thanks, Tivia."

After a pause she added, "For a man, that is." But there wasn't the usual haughtiness in her voice as she said it. "You surprise me."

"Well, gee, I appreciate that, Tivia. I'm glad I was able to surprise you." Then, because he knew it would bug her, he added, "So do we kiss and make up?"

And then, to his utter shock, he felt her lips press briefly against his cheek. She had lowered her mask just for a moment and by the time he had turned, it was already back in place along with her usual inscrutable expression. "You're not the only one capable of surprises, Bhodi Li. Remember that."

"You—you kissed me!"

"I did no such thing. I think your fantasies are starting to run away with you, Bhodi. Parcival, did you see me come anywhere near Bhodi?"

"Me?" said Parcival innocently. "Of course not. Don't be ridiculous."

Bhodi moaned softly. "Leon will never believe it. No one will."

There was a sudden knocking on the trapdoor beneath their feet.

Bhodi and Tivia immediately brought their Phasers to bear and Parcival, who was carrying his baseball bat in one hand, swung it around in readiness. But they all relaxed when the knocking took on the "all-clear" tap that Gretta had briefed them on. Still they waited until they heard her say, "Are you up there?"

"Yeah. Hold on." Bhodi moved aside the trapdoor and they each dropped lightly to the ground. Bhodi looked at her anxiously. "Are you okay? They didn't threaten you or anything?"

She laughed. "It was a false alarm, my friends. It was indeed the Gestapo, but he was on our side."

"What?"

She gestured for them to follow her, and they went down to the living room as she spoke. "The underground has several people infiltrated into the Gestapo, the SS, the Vermacht—even Hitler's personal guard. The Fuehrer leads a charmed life that he has survived as long as he has. I put out feelers about the ones you seek and one of our covert people was reporting back to me. However, it wouldn't have looked good for a member of the Gestapo to just come up to my door in any sort of informal manner. So he pounded loudly, made a great show of his coming here."

Bhodi and Parcival sat in chairs while Tivia crouched near the door, as if ready to move should the slightest danger arise. "What did he tell you?"

"The three you describe—they are definitely in the hands of the Gestapo."

"Well, sure, we knew that." Bhodi described how they had spotted Mandarr in the back of the truck.

Gretta nodded. "Did you see the other two in there as well?"

"I'm not sure. They might have been in the truck, but it was dark and the thing was moving so quickly—I just can't be certain. So for all we know, Pirarr and Destructarr are still back at the Gestapo headquarters."

"Mandarr might be there, too," said Parcival reasonably. "After all, we don't know for certain where he was being taken."

"He's right," admitted Bhodi. "So what do we do?"

"The answer is obvious," said Tivia, straightening up and walking gingerly around the bits of radio still spread out on the floor. "We break into the headquarters of the Gestapo, blast those three walking creep shows back to Arr and then get out of this backwater era."

"Works for me," said Bhodi Li.

"Me too," said Parcival.

Bhodi stood and said, "Gretta. We're going to need raincoats and headgear again to go out. Scarves particularly for Parcival and Tivia. Gloves too, if possible."

"Easily possible." She paused. "I have some pancake makeup upstairs. Would you like me to apply it to them to try and lighten their skin?"

Bhodi looked at Parcival and Tivia, who appeared uncomfortable at the suggestion. But before he could say anything, Tivia nodded briskly. "That would probably be for the best," she said. "Something so that we would escape detection upon a casual glance. All right with you, Parcival?"

Parcival shrugged. "A Photon Guardian's got to do what a Photon Guardian's got to do."

An hour later, decked out in raingear and appropriately made up, the three Photon Warriors went out. The rain had slowed to a drizzle now, and Parcival and Tivia kept their hats pulled down low to prevent the makeup from washing off. Bhodi could barely see their eyes peering out from beneath the hats and above the scarves they wore.

As she watched the three of them walk away, Gretta could not help but recall what else the Gestapo contact had told her.

"Watch yourself, Gretta. The Gestapo is very concerned about a number of people these days, and I believe that you are one of those they are keeping an eye on."

"I can't stop doing what I know is right," she had replied.

"I'm aware of that, Gretta," he had said patiently. "But by the same token I don't want you getting yourself killed. Just be careful. That's all I'm asking."

And as she watched the three of them disappear around the corner, she wondered if they would ever come back. And if they did, would she be there to greet them?

10
Breaking and Entering

They stood a block away from Gestapo headquarters, surveying it with cool efficiency. "We could jump the wall around it," offered Tivia. "That would be no problem."

"Yeah. But the dogs inside would be a problem. Even if we take them out—"

"Which we can," said Parcival.

"They'd still alert the entire place to our presence."

"All right," said Tivia. "What's your idea?"

"It'll come to me," said Bhodi. "It'll come to me."

"Excuse me."

They all turned. A Gestapo man, in his ominous hat and black coat with the bright red swastika armband, surveyed them critically. "May I ask what your business is here?"

Bhodi glanced up and down the street. There was no one around. He looked at Tivia and a slow smile spread across his face. "Tivia—it just came to me."

The Gestapo man looked at them, frowning. "What are you talking about? I want to see your identification. Now."

The Gestapo had become used to instant obedience. Everyone throughout Germany, and much of the world for that matter, feared and respected the Gestapo. When the Gestapo said jump, the response was not "Why?" but "How high?" So the thought that the three people in front of him would do other than meekly comply never crossed his mind. Which was too bad for him.

It happened too quickly for even Bhodi to follow, and he'd been expecting it. Tivia's hand lashed out, a sharp karate blow to the base of the man's neck. She followed with a fast right to the jaw and consciousness slipped away from him. He started to sag to the ground but Bhodi caught him before he was more than halfway there. Another quick glance to make sure no one was around, and then the three Photon Warriors dragged their prize into a nearby alleyway.

Bhodi gave him the quick once-over. "He's about my size. He'll do." He started to remove his coat.

"Bhodi, don't tell me you're thinking of doing what I know you're thinking of doing," said Parcival.

"Okay. I won't. Now get his uniform off him. Tivia, I'd be much obliged if you'd turn around."

'I think that would be best," said Tivia, turning on her heel.

She heard the rustling of clothes behind her but wasn't the least bit tempted to turn around until Bhodi said, "Okay. How do I look?"

She turned and gasped slightly. The friendly-looking young man named Bhodi Li was gone. In his place was a fierce looking Gestapo man who seemed to bear only a passing resemblance to the Photon Guardian. His armor lay in a neat pile on the ground, and the Gestapo man they'd ambushed was wrapped up in the coat Bhodi had been wearing.

"You look . . . very convincing. Like a real Nazi."

"I don't know if that's exactly a compliment, but thanks anyway." He reached down to the holster and pulled out the Walther PPK gingerly. He extended the butt to Parcival, who took it with no more enthusiasm than Bhodi offered it. Tivia in turn took the gun from Parcival and studied it.

"Primitive weapon," she observed.

"Careful!" said Bhodi. "Don't hurt—"

Without warning, Tivia spun the pistol expertly on her finger like a cowboy. She twirled it and then brought it to a halt, barrel pointing upward. "Well weighted, though."

"—yourself," Bhodi finished weakly. Then he reached down to his Photon gear and pulled his Phaser from its holster, sliding it into the holster of his new uniform. It was bigger than the other gun, but with the coat over it he doubted it would be noticed.

"Wish me luck," he said.

"Bhodi, this is a really idiotic idea," said Parcival. Tivia nodded absently, still studying the gun.

Bhodi shrugged. "Well, that's not exactly luck, but it'll have to do. If I run into trouble, I'll send up a flare. You keep your eyes on sleeping beauty here."

"Got it."

Bhodi started towards Gestapo headquarters. After a dozen paces he turned and looked back, but Tivia and Parcival were already hiding in the alley. He smiled. Always cautious, those two. He pulled his hat down by the brim as far as it would go and walked with slow steps towards the outer gate.

It was a large, elaborate affair, and there was a fierce-looking guard there with an equally fierce-looking Doberman. Bhodi paused only a moment to recheck the comforting shape of his Phaser under his coat, and then strode forward with an uncertain conviction.

Just as he got to the gate he remembered how his grandfather had told him Nazis always greeted each other. He stopped a few feet from the guard, snapped his hand upward, and said in as deep a voice as he could muster "Heil Hitler."

"Heil Hitler," was the immediate reply, and Bhodi relaxed a little. Then the guard said, "What are your orders?"

Bhodi blinked and then, trying to maintain his assertiveness, said, "Bring me inside, and make it quick."

The guard looked at him in surprise and Bhodi knew that he had completely misunderstood what the guard was asking. In a low, warning tone the Doberman growled at him. His lip curling in a feral sneer, Bhodi growled right back. The dog immediately shut up.

"You are making some sort of joke, Herr . . ." He waited for Bhodi to fill in the name. Bhodi quickly tried to think of a German surname and came up with the only one that occurred to him.

"Klink," said Bhodi. "Colonel Klink."

"Herr Colonel, this was some sort of joke?"

"Yes, a joke," said Bhodi. It was only then that he realized that, as he concentrated on speaking the language, his American accent had completely disappeared. Apparently the longer he was there the more accustomed he became to speaking German. He wondered, if he stayed there long enough, would he forget how to speak English completely? But then he saw the guard was waiting, and he continued quickly, "That's me. I joke sometimes. They say we Germans have no sense of humor."

"I always felt that was a fair assessment," said the guard stiffly. He looked down unhappily to see that the Doberman was eyeing Bhodi with clear nervousness. "I am still waiting, Herr Colonel, for your orders. What is your business here?"

"My business!" said Bhodi as if a fog had just been pierced. "Of course. Foolish of me; I should have realized immediately what you meant. I have my orders right here."

He reached into the inside of his coat, sliding his hand down towards his Phaser. This was not how he had wanted to get in, but it now seemed he had no choice. But then, just before his hand gripped the butt of his pistol, his searching fingers found a pocket on the inside of his coat. In the pocket were several pieces of paper, folded into thirds. Bhodi paused a moment, surprised but trying not to let it show. Then he slowly pulled the papers out and handed them wordlessly to the guard.

The guard nodded slowly, scrutinizing the papers, and then he handed the papers back and saluted smartly. "All is in order, Herr Colonel. Heil Hitler."

Bhodi rocked back slightly on his heels as he slid the orders back into the pocket. "Heil Hitler," he responded, and walked boldly through the gates. Before he'd gone more than a few steps, however, he heard the guard call "Herr Klink."

Bhodi froze, waiting for a gunshot or a bullet in the back. When neither was forthcoming, he slowly turned to see the guard standing there, looking as if he was trying to force a smile.

"Your joke was very amusing," said the guard stiffly.

Bhodi inclined his head slightly as acknowledgment, stifling an urge to laugh out loud. "I'm glad I was able to amuse you, mein Herr." Then he turned and walked across the courtyard to the main entrance of Gestapo headquarters.

He entered the main area, which was large and elaborate. The first thing that caught his eye was the huge portrait of Adolf Hitler hanging in the foyer. The second thing that he saw was the bust of Hitler that sat on a pedestal under the painting. Slowly he shook his head. The man practically radiated evil. When in a dull old history class he had looked at pictures of this man, it had seemed pointless. Who cared? He was dead and gone, and, besides, he looked like pictures of Charlie Chaplin that Bhodi had once seen. How could the entire world have been afraid of a man who looked like Charlie Chaplin?

But now, staring at that malevolent gaze, Bhodi could

almost feel the evil of the man, and it chilled him to his bone that this man was alive somewhere, plotting more horrors, waging war and slaughtering millions of innocent people.

"Heil Hitler!"

Bhodi turned quickly and saw another Gestapo man looking at him with carefully maintained politeness. Immediately all business, Bhodi snapped a salute back. "Heil Hitler."

"May I help you, mein Herr?"

"Yes," said Bhodi with brisk authority. "I am looking for the commanding officer. His name is . . ." Without missing a beat, Bhodi snapped his fingers in irritation as if searching his memory for a forgotten name.

Bhodi was lucky in that the Gestapo man he was facing was somewhat new and a little slow off the mark. "Colonel Schliss?" he offered helpfully.

Bhodi snapped once and pointed triumphantly. "Yes! That's his name. Colonel Schliss. Where is he?"

"In his office," said the Gestapo man smartly.

"And that would be—?"

He pointed to the spiral stairs at the far end of the foyer. "Up the stairs, second door on the right."

"Thank you," said Bhodi. "You have been most kind."

"My pleasure, Herr Colonel. Heil Hitler."

"Heil Hitler," was Bhodi's reply. At first the phrase had been difficult for him to say—the moral aspects were overwhelming. But with the constant repetition the unthinkable had quickly become the routine.

He followed the directions he had been given and moments later was standing in front of a large set of double doors. Taking a breath he knocked briskly.

From within came an impatient "Yes?"

"Colonel Schliss?" he called through the door.

"Yes, what is it? I am very involved with several important projects right now."

Bhodi called, "It's quite important, colonel. Almost a matter of life and death, you might say."

There was an annoyed sigh from inside, and then he called, "Make it quick."

Bhodi smiled as he pushed open the door and stepped inside. He was immediately struck by the length of the office. With a few obstacles and some fog, this place was big enough to be a Photon arena.

Schliss looked up impatiently from a pile of paperwork on his desk. "Yes? You said a matter of life and death? Whose?"

Bhodi had unbuttoned his coat, allowing it to hang open. Time to come on strong, he thought, and he reached into his coat and pulled out his Phaser. With his best Clint Eastwood voice Bhodi said, "Yours."

Schliss stared down the long room at him in disbelief. "You would barge into Gestapo headquarters," he said, carefully measuring each word, "and threaten me, a colonel in the Gestapo—with a toy gun? You are mad." Totally uncowed the colonel reached towards the phone on his right. "I'm calling security and having you escorted out. You have that much time to say your prayers."

It never even seemed as if Bhodi was aiming. He pointed his Phaser with stunning casualness and squeezed off a shot. A pencil-thin beam of light streaked across the room and lanced through the telephone unit. Schliss sat there in stunned silence as the phone unit melted into a puddle on his desktop. The receiver he held in his hand was now completely dead. For all he knew, he would be next.

That Bhodi would not fire the Phaser at him never occurred to Schliss. The common-sense thinking in the Gestapo was, if you had a weapon, you use it. It was this mentality on which Bhodi was counting.

"Put down the receiver," Bhodi said evenly. "Now."

Never taking his eyes from Bhodi, Colonel Schliss slowly placed the receiver back in the remains of its cradle. Then he waited.

"I want information," said Bhodi.

"You won't get it," replied Schliss.

Bhodi fired again and this time the laser beam sliced through a bust of Hitler off to Schliss's left. The top half of Hitler's head came loose and fell to the ground, shattering.

"By hook or by crook, I will," Bhodi said with a low voice.

Schliss stared at the broken bust, the melted phone, and then said, "What do you wish to know?"

Bhodi walked slowly towards him, the barrel of his Phaser never wavering. "Mandarr. Pirarr. Destructarr. Where are they?"

Schliss nodded in understanding. "You're one of theirs."

Bhodi stared at him. "One of theirs what?"

"I should have recognized the weapon immediately. I will tell you what you wish to know . . . but you must tell me. What country are you from?"

"Classified, colonel."

Schliss paused. "The Fuehrer believes that your friends . . . no, I sense that friends is not the right word . . . those you seek are supernatural in origin. The Fuehrer has a great belief in the supernatural. Tell me that, at least."

With a shrug, Bhodi said, "All right. No. We're not supernatural if by that you mean ghosts or that sort of thing."

"Elder gods, as the Fuehrer calls them?"

"A god?" Bhodi almost laughed. "I'm practically flunking algebra. How could I be a god?"

"Well . . . whatever you are, if I tell you where those you seek are, will you find them and leave with them?"

Bhodi nodded. "Bet on it."

"Good. You must understand, my young friend . . . this is my second war. And I am of the firm opinion that men's wars should be fought by men. Creatures such as . . . which one was the monstrous one?"

"Destructarr."

"Yes. Destructarr, as I was saying, has no place in our war. I could, of course, be tried for treason for these things. But I am the old-fashioned sort. I don't want you or those freaks butting into our war. When the Germans win, it will be because we are the superior race. Not because we had aid from those freaks.''

Bhodi waved his Phaser. "Talk is cheap, colonel. I don't want your personal philosophy on warfare. I want the guys I'm looking for.''

For reply, Schliss reached into his drawer and pulled out a map, which he unfolded with brisk efficiency. He gestured and Bhodi walked cautiously over to him, never dropping his guard. But Schliss seemed to have lost interest completely in the Phaser. "How well," he asked, "do you know Berlin and the surrounding area?''

"Not all that much," admitted Bhodi.

He nodded. "All right. The ones you're looking for have been taken to Hitler's headquarters, which is here." With a pencil he circled a spot on the map. "We," he added, "are here," and he circled Gestapo headquarters' location.

Bhodi nodded. "Can you get me in there?''

Schliss stared at him with open amusement. "Possibly. But I won't. Because if you succeed in your mission and take away the Fuehrer's latest . . . acquisitions . . . it will be remembered that you were brought in at my behest.'' He laughed unpleasantly. "I would not last twenty-four hours. And I wish to last a great deal longer than that. Gaining entrance is your problem. But I can assure you that it's going to be quite a bit more difficult than getting in here. Quite a bit more difficult.''

Bhodi nodded. "All right. That pretty much tells me what I need to know." Then he paused. "I guess I'll have to tie you up or something.''

"That is inefficient. That is why we shall eventually triumph—because we alone think in an efficient, organized manner.'' He turned his back to Bhodi and pointed to the back of his head. "Right about here should do the job. Not only will it be to my advantage to be found unconscious, allowing you sufficient time to escape, but any memory loss I may suffer as to what I told you will be substantiated.''

Bhodi nodded. He gripped his Phaser by the barrel and swung it once, smacking Schliss resoundingly on the back of the head. Schliss went down without a word, dropping like a sack of wheat. Bhodi started to pick him up to put him in his chair and then decided against it. He didn't want to appear too concerned—it might serve to go against whatever story Schliss made up to cover himself.

I'm concerned about a Nazi, thought Bhodi in wonderment. Boy, wouldn't Grandpa be ticked off about that?

He glanced at the top of Schliss's desk. Everything in neat, efficient piles. Very impressive.

And then he saw something that he would later swear caused his heart to stop beating for a moment.

Numb, he picked up a piece of paper. It was a list of names, all neatly typed. He did not know whether the device in his head enabled him to read German in addition to speaking it, but it wouldn't have been necessary in this case. There was a single word written across the top, a word which said it all. A name.

''Dachau.''

And on the list of names, fourth from the top, was Gretta's.

11

A Matter of Priorities

The Gestapo man who had been knocked out in the alley slowly moaned as he tried to sit up. Through the haze of his semiconsciousness he heard the voice of a young boy say, "Our friend's starting to come to."

Then he felt something like a vise clamp on the back of his neck. And he dropped back into the blackness of unconsciousness.

"Not bad," Parcival said as Tivia stood up, removing her hand from the man's neck. "Mr. Spock would be proud."

Tivia glanced over at him. "Who?"

"Skip it." He paused. "It's been over an hour. How do you think Bhodi is doing?"

"Fine, I'm sure. I'm not concerned."

Parcival looked at her skeptically. "Tivia, we've been through a lot together. I feel that I can give my input here."

"On what, Parcival?"

"To be blunt—whom are you kidding? All of us can tell that you're really stuck on Bhodi."

"Nonsense."

"It's not nonsense. I don't deal in nonsense. I deal in facts, data that can be distilled and analyzed. And all the data point to the same conclusion."

"Well, it's the wrong conclusion," she said petulantly, leaning against a wall. "Even if I were interested in a man, which is patently impossible, it wouldn't be someone like Bhodi. He'd have to be someone whom I could respect. Someone I . . . liked. I don't like Bhodi."

Parcival raised an eyebrow over the top of his round glasses. "You don't? Not the least little bit?"

"All right," she allowed. "The least little bit. But he's so . . . irritating. I can remember dozens of things he's done in the time that I've known him that irritate me beyond belief."

"But don't you understand, Tivia? It wouldn't be nearly so annoying to you if you didn't care so much."

She actually seemed amused. "Are you saying that you know I like him because I dislike him so much?"

"I know it sounds contradictory, but emotions frequently are. Maybe that's why Lord Baethan's people have pretty much eliminated them. Right?"

"Perhaps Baethan has the right idea," murmured Tivia. "Feelings are so confusing. That's part of the reason that men are forbidden on my planet."

"You mean it's not just that women are supposed to be so much better?" said Parcival.

Still smarting from Bhodi's earlier comments on that subject, Tivia said, "Putting that aside. It's because we women pride ourselves on our fighting skills and strength. Emotional entanglements sap the strength, clutter the concentration. We wanted to dispense with all that." She was silent for a time and then she muttered something.

"I'm sorry, Tivia," said Parcival. "I didn't quite catch that. Sounds to me like you said, 'Maybe we were wrong.' "

"Nonsense. I said, 'I hope it won't be too long.' About Bhodi returning, I mean."

Parcival peered around the corner and grinned. "Wishes come true sometimes. Here he comes."

Tivia joined Parcival and watched Bhodi's approach. They noticed at the same time that Bhodi's face had gone deadly white, as if he'd been told that his mother had just died. Instead of the usual smooth flow of his movements, Bhodi's steps were leaden.

"Something's wrong," said Tivia. "He must not have found out where the Dark Guardians are."

Parcival shook his head. "No. It's something more serious than that. Just look at him. He looks like death warmed over."

They waited until he got closer and then Parcival hissed, "Bhodi!"

Bhodi looked up as if he were seeing them for the first time. Then, as if something had been triggered within him, Bhodi walked with new determination to his friends. Before they could say anything, Bhodi pulled a piece of paper out of his pocket and thrust it at them. Tivia took it and stared at it. "Dachau? What's that?"

"It's a concentration camp."

Tivia blinked. "Well, concentration is good for the spirit," she said uncertainly.

"It's a euphemism," said Bhodi. "It's really a death camp. Grandpa says they exterminated millions of people in places like that."

Tivia gasped. "Millions? We don't have millions of people on our entire planet!"

"Yeah. And Dachau was one of the worst of the death camps."

"Bhodi, this is all very interesting," said Parcival. "But I don't quite see how that's particularly pertinent. Did you find out about Mandarr and the rest?"

"Yeah, yeah. They're at Hitler's headquarters. But that's not important now."

"Not important?" exclaimed Tivia. "If that's not, what is? We have to get over there immediately."

"Look at this list! See anybody familiar on there?"

Tivia looked at it again and this time she saw. "Oh dear." She pointed out Gretta's name to Parcival, who observed, "There's a date next to her name. Today's date."

"We've got to help her!" said Bhodi. "Come on." He grabbed up his armor and started putting it on. Tivia automatically averted her gaze as she said, "Bhodi, there's a problem."

"Darn right there's a problem!" said Bhodi. "They want to ace Gretta. She stuck her neck out for us and we have to do the same for her. We're the good guys. That's what we do."

Parcival said, "Bhodi—we're supposed to interfere as little as possible. If history says that Gretta is supposed to be arrested then, as painful as that may be, we have to let that happen."

Bhodi turned, fully armored, eyes wide. "Are you nuts? What good is our power if we can't use it to save one woman?"

"We're trying to save an entire planet," said Tivia in no uncertain terms. "Perhaps an entire galaxy. Cold as it may seem, Bhodi, one life pales into insignificance compared to that."

"Oh, that's great! That's just great! Some friends you are."

"Bhodi," Tivia put a hand on his shoulder but he pulled away. She persisted, "We have no time to waste. Parcival, do you have the transportation device MOM gave us?"

Parcival reached under his vest and pulled out the cylindrical machine. "Right here. It's a marvelous machine, really. You can either set it to coordinates, or you can use the recall link. If you've been somewhere and can picture it in your mind, it'll take you there.''

"You're really serious about this!" said Bhodi. "You're really not going to do anything to help Gretta."

"If we could, we would," said Tivia. "But you have to have your priorities straight, Bhodi Li."

"Well, maybe I'm the only one who does!" shouted Bhodi. With a lunge so swift that he was practically invisible, Bhodi grabbed the transportation device from Parcival's grasp. He backpedaled quickly out of Tivia's and Parcival's reach.

"Bhodi Li, don't do it!" shouted Parcival. But Tivia had already dug into her belt and removed a star blade. Even as Bhodi turned the cylinder's top, she hurled the blade at his hand, hoping to knock the transporter out of it.

She was a split second too slow. A cone of blue light surrounded him and with a quick twist Bhodi Li vanished into the air.

"Well, that's just wonderful!" raged Tivia. "He's done it again. He's always doing this, running off half-baked and forgetting what's important."

Parcival was silent. Tivia turned to him. "Say something! Don't you agree?"

"I agree that Bhodi is impetuous," said Parcival. "But to be perfectly honest, I understand how he feels. Would it really be so terrible if we tried to save her?"

"I . . . I don't know. We're not supposed to meddle . . ."

"No one knows everything there is to know about time travel," said Parcival reasonably. "You could argue that the past is already past, and anything that we would want to do, we've already done. That it's all meant to happen. That all we can do is what we believe to be right at the given moment."

Tivia was silent. Then she said, "All right. Let's go get Gretta out of whatever trouble she's in. But Parcival— when I get my hands on Bhodi, I'm still going to wring his neck!"

*   *   *

In a burst of blue light Bhodi materialized on the front steps of Gretta's house. Several passersby jumped in surprise but Bhodi was beyond caring. He bounded up the steps and kicked open the door.

"Gretta!" he shouted. "Gretta, you have to get out!"

But even before the echo of his words had died out, he knew that he had arrived too late. Pieces of leftover radio lay strewn on the floor where Parcival had left them in his futile attempts to fix his shattered computer. But they had all been smashed flat. Bhodi knew why—the booted feet of the soldiers had crushed them. The soldiers who had come to take Gretta away.

He had one desperate hope. He ran up the narrow steps to the attic and, barely slowing down, leaped up into the hidden attic. But she wasn't there.

He ran downstairs again, shouting her name, hoping against hope. Standing in the living room, fighting back the fury and misery that threatened to overwhelm him, Bhodi felt his stomach tighten into a knot. He wasn't going to give up. Tivia and Parcival were not going to be right about this. He wasn't going to give in to history.

He reached into a closet, pulled out the last remaining coat and tossed it over his armor. He didn't even bother to button it as he darted out into the street. He took a step back and faced the neighboring houses.

An older man was peering out through a window on the second floor of the next-door house. His eyes met Bhodi's intense gaze and he quickly moved away from the window. But that wasn't going to stop Bhodi—not in his mood. With the Photon energy in his legs he leaped upward and smashed through the window, shielding his face with his arms. He was in the old man's bedroom. The old man had just lain down on the bed, a book balanced on his stomach. His jaw dropped and he rolled off the bed, starting to make for the door.

His feet crunching on the glass, Bhodi had jumped in

front of the door before the old man had cleared the mattress. He froze, saw the look in Bhodi's face, and tried to stutter something out. Bhodi stepped right up to him, shoved his face in the old man's, and said, "Where is she?"

The mouth moved without words for a moment and then he said, "I . . . I don't know what you mean."

"You know exactly what I mean. Gretta Meuller. Your next-door neighbor. Where is she?"

He tried to look away. "I don't know anything. I haven't seen anything."

But Bhodi grabbed him by the chin and swung his head around to face him. "Oh no you don't. You're not turning away this time. My Grandpa told me how everybody just sat back and looked away and let it all happen. But you're not going to let this happen. You hear?" With one hand he lifted the old man so high that his head almost hit the ceiling. "You're not going to let this happen!"

"All right!" His voice had gone so high it was practically a shriek. "I saw them take her away. The soldiers. They were rounding up a lot of people. I saw them shove her into a truck."

"Where did they take her?" When the answer was not immediately forthcoming, he shook the man once more. "Where?!"

"I'm not sure!" shrieked the man. "Probably to the trainyards. That's where they've taken everyone else. They put them on the trains and they take them off to be relocated."

"Relocated?" Bhodi could barely hide his disgust as he let the old man drop to the floor. "Are you that blind? They're taking them off to be killed. Slaughtered like cattle."

"No." The old man shook his head furiously. "No, that's crazy. You're saying crazy things. They're not—"

"They are."

"But they wouldn't . . ."

"They have and they will and they'll keep on doing it, and you and all the others just stand by until it's too late."

The old man kept on shaking his head and Bhodi, with a sigh, pulled out his map. He unfolded it and said, "Show me. Here on the map."

With a trembling finger the old man pointed. Bhodi studied it, then removed the transportation cylinder from where he'd tucked it in his chest armor. He stared at the cylinder, the map, back at the cylinder, and then came to the depressing realization that he didn't have the faintest idea how to set it to a coordinate. There was a small array of numbers and dials on the bottom, but he didn't know how to key them in.

He turned to the old man. "Can you see the trainyard from here?"

The old man nodded. Grabbing him by the scruff of his neck Bhodi dragged the man over to the window and said, "Show me."

The old man extended an arm, indicating a point so far in the distance that Bhodi had to squint to see it. "That it way out there?"

"Yes."

Suddenly Bhodi heard the sound of pounding feet. Several soldiers were running toward the house, pointing up at him. Clearly good news traveled fast, and Bhodi's effortless leap through the window had obviously brought the authorities running.

Well, the devil with them.

He focused his full attention on the far-off trainyard, twisted the cylinder, and felt the house fall away from him.

"Uh oh." Parcival drew himself up short. "Did you see it?"

"See what?"

"A quick blue flash. Over the top of the buildings. Energy surge."

Tivia winced. "He transported again? But MOM said that we could only use it three times, before the power goes out."

"And we've had a firsthand example of what happens if we try to power up our instruments with the local current."

"So what do we do?" demanded Tivia. "It seemed reasonable that he was heading to Gretta's house. But now we have no idea where he went."

Parcival looked at his wrist computer unit. "I've got an idea, Tivia. It's going to take me a little time to put together. We'll approach Gretta's house slowly. If there are any soldiers around, we'll wait until they leave, and then we'll go in and cobble together whatever we can find."

Tivia shook her head. "I can't believe that Bhodi is putting us through this. It's so . . . so . . ."

"Human?" offered Parcival.

She looked at him and there was amusement in her eyes. "Yes. It's that. It's most definitely that."

12

Von Bhodi's Express

It was a freight train, with human cattle.

Bhodi materialized just in time to see the train lurch forward from the station. It was eight cars long with an old-fashioned (there was that wrongheaded thinking again!) engine puffing away. The terrified screams and low moans from the people in the cars were the first things that hit Bhodi, and he felt a deep sickness in his stomach.

It occurred to him that the monsters he had met in his battles were nothing compared to the monsters being spewed out by the Third Reich.

A couple of stray guards stood around watching dispassionately as the train pulled out of the weatherbeaten station. The doors on each of the freight cars were closed and locked, but they were not solid. Instead they were composed of horizontal slats, and Bhodi could see, between the slats, the tragedy in the people's faces. Old faces. Young faces. Men and women and children. Kids who were Bhodi's age.

He did not see Gretta. He didn't have to. He could almost sense her presence. She was in there, shoved in among the people somewhere. People on top of one another, crying, pleading for help . . .

"Don't move!"

Bhodi spun. A soldier was behind him, his gun aimed point-blank at Bhodi's stomach.

"I said don't move!" repeated the soldier. Then he raised his voice and shouted to two companions standing near the tracks. "Over here! Quick—"

Bhodi moved. Seething with rage, he had now found an outlet. He grabbed the barrel of the gun with both hands and shoved forward. The rifle stock rammed into the soldier's stomach, knocking the breath out of him. The soldier lost his grip on the gun, and Bhodi yanked it from his hands, tossed it aside, then stepped forward and delivered a roundhouse to the point of the soldier's chin.

Even as he lapsed into unconsciousness, his friends charged forward, rifles at the ready. Without pause Bhodi scooped up the soldier, lifted him overhead and hurled the limp body at the oncoming pair. They tried to backpedal but they weren't fast enough. They went down in a heap and before they could get up, Bhodi Li was on top of them.

He had to restrain himself. His heart pumped furiously. He would have knocked their heads off if he'd given in to the anger, but he had more self-control than that. He satisfied himself with sending them to dreamland.

He looked up frantically. The last car of the train was already many yards off and gaining speed. He started to run, shucking the coat entirely. He had recovered his helmet back at Gretta's and attached it to his belt. Now, on the run, he detached it from the belt and slapped it on his head. His Phaser was still in his holster. He wouldn't need it yet. All he needed now was speed.

In the past forty-eight hours he had gotten barely eight hours sleep, but he wasn't at all tired. He ran, his legs scissoring, his arms driving him forward. He leaped onto the railroad track and started running harder, closing in. The rear car, the caboose, was getting closer. He pounded faster, his helmet jiggling on his head, his holster slapping against his thigh. He had no idea how fast he was going, but the ground beneath his feet was streaking by.

They were leaving the city behind, and Bhodi was now lagging behind only a couple of yards. But the train was picking up speed and, as his desperate arm stretched out to the back railing on the caboose, it started to pull farther away from him.

No! he screamed desperately in his mind. And the desperate thought translated to desperate action. Gathering all the power that his energized body possessed, Bhodi leaped, every muscle in his body straining.

One hand snagged the railing. For several agonizing seconds Bhodi was dragged behind the train, unable to get his legs or other arm up. With a grunt Bhodi swung his left arm up, and now he was holding on with both hands, and in another second he had pulled himself halfway up onto the small platform on the rear of the caboose. If he had had yet another second, he would have been able to swing both his legs up and over.

Unfortunately another second was exactly what he didn't have.

A soldier stepped out, in the middle of taking a long drag on a cigarette. He froze, his gaze locking with Bhodi's, and his mouth dropped open. The cigarette plopped out, skidded off the platform and fell off. The train left it far behind.

"Give me a hand!" shouted Bhodi.

And the guard, still not quite understanding what was happening, reached down and hauled Bhodi up onto the platform of the caboose.

"Thanks," said Bhodi, and with a quick jab he knocked the soldier cold, turned, and hurled him off the train. The soldier landed on the flat plain that surrounded them.

The train was starting to move even faster now, rolling at about thirty miles an hour. Bhodi peered in through the small door that led to the interior of the caboose.

A dozen soldiers lounged around, smoking cigarettes or chatting amiably with each other. Odd, thought Bhodi. They looked so normal now, not like monsters at all. Again, many of them looked about his own age. It was hard to understand. The bad guys were supposed to have fangs or horns. They should look evil, not . . . ordinary.

Bhodi didn't want to think about it anymore. He also didn't want to deal with having to fight all these guys. He didn't want to slug it out with soldiers; he wanted to set Gretta and the others free.

He wished that Parcival were there. Parcival was the strategist of the Photon Warriors. Parcival would have come up with half a dozen ways to handle this with a minimum of muss and fuss. And Baethan, he of the cold logic. He would have been able to calmly assess the situation and make a logical, rational decision. He wouldn't have gone off on this half-cocked.

What would Baethan and Parcival do?

If you can't go through an obstacle, then go around or over it.

He looked up and, within a moment of assessing the situation, he had developed a plan. He was eminently pleased with himself.

He stepped away from the small door, reached up and got a grip on the roof of the caboose. Effortlessly he swung upward and within seconds had clambered to the roof, as silently as he could. He paused there a few moments, his arms outstretched to keep his balance, to see if there was any reaction from beneath his feet. But he heard nothing and was satisfied that no one in the car had heard him.

His plan was simple. As he made his way to the front of the train, he would use his Phaser to blast off the large padlocks that imprisoned the people in the cars. Then, once he got to the front, he would sever the coupling that held the train to the engine. The engine would go on its merry way, leaving the rest of the train far behind. The people would then have at least a chance of survival. Granted not a great chance, but better than they had now.

It was a simple plan, an elegant plan.

As he reached the midway point of the caboose, the roof gave way and suddenly his right leg had gone through up to his knee. He heard shouts of surprise from below him, cursed under his breath and pulled his leg out. He didn't even stop to look down the hole that was now in the roof. He dashed forward, breathing a quick prayer that nothing else would fall apart beneath him. He got to the edge of the caboose and leaped to the next car.

Even though there was no fancy platform, there was still a door on this end of the caboose. A door which was now flung open, and a soldier filled it. But Bhodi already had his Phaser out and with one clean shot he sliced through the coupling that held the caboose to the train. With a lurch the caboose came free of the train. Bhodi dropped flat to his stomach as a bullet cracked over his head. Giving in to impulse, he stuck his tongue out at the frustrated soldier, who was already becoming smaller and smaller in the distance. All the soldiers were pouring out of the freed caboose, and they were firing their rifles desperately.

Bhodi was puzzled. He was already drawing out of range, yet a number of soldiers were simply firing straight up, as if they weren't concerned about hitting him. As if he wasn't their target.

Bhodi shrugged. It didn't matter. So he had hit an unexpected hitch in his plan right at the beginning. Big deal. Everything was going to go smooth as silk now.

He made his way along the roof of a car that had people crammed into it. Getting to the center, he lay down on his stomach, his head hanging over the edge of the car, and slowly eased his way forward until he was able to see into it.

People looked at him in astonishment. They were packed in like sardines, and it was so dark he could hardly see. He called as loudly as he could, "Gretta! Gretta Meuller!" The wind whipped by him, carrying his words away as he shouted again and again. When he heard no response, he forced himself to mentally shrug. Well, there were seven other cars as well to check. He took aim and blasted off the padlocks on either side that held the gate closed. The people inside gasped as they saw the beam of light flash out and effortlessly strike away that which was imprisoning them.

And then Bhodi was about to move to the next car when he heard a voice call out from within, "Bhodi?"

He could scarcely believe his luck. "Gretta!"

Pushing as hard, as unyieldingly as she could, Gretta forced her way to the front. Her face was filled with joy and she reached out through the bars of the door to him. He grabbed his hand in hers, their fingers intertwining for a moment. "I thought I'd never see you again!" she half sobbed.

"You won't," Bhodi yelled. "I'll get you loose, and then the rest is up to you."

For a moment hopelessness and despair filled her face. But only for a moment, and then she wadded up the useless emotions like scrap paper and tossed them away. These would not help her now, and her face set in determined lines. "As many of us who can escape, will," she said. "Bhodi . . . you're going to be a tough act to follow."

Bhodi grinned, squeezed her hand once more, and pulled himself back up to the roof.

A shot whizzed over his head.

He stayed flat on his stomach, looking in the direction that the shot had come from. At the far end of the train, near the engine, soldiers were slowly approaching him along the top of the speeding train. Bhodi realized now why the soldiers had fired into the air—they were alerting their co-workers, who must have been up in the front.

"Nuts!" cried Bhodi. He swung around, dropped his legs over the edge and started to climb down the side of the car, clinging onto the horizontal slats of the door for dear life. Gretta was looking at him in confusion.

Bhodi continued to climb down, closer to the ground, until it was zipping along right under his booted feet. Taking a deep breath, Bhodi swung himself down, working and squirming his way under until he was clinging, batlike, to the underside of the car.

The speeding track was bare inches beneath him and he had to arch his back so as not to have the skin ripped off his backside. He pulled his way forward, inch by agonizing inch. The car shook as if trying to throw him off, but he wouldn't release his grip. He slithered forward until he reached the edge of the car.

Twisting and turning like a contortionist, Bhodi wrapped himself around the coupling that attached Gretta's car to the next. He pulled himself up and for a moment he hesitated. If he severed the coupling while he was on this side, the rest of the train would go speeding off, leaving himself and Gretta's car. He need not risk himself further.

And the rest of the train would go speeding off, carrying seven cars full of people to certain death.

Into the darkness.

"The light shines," murmured Bhodi, and swung himself over to the other side. He unholstered his Phaser, aimed downward and blasted the coupling free.

The train, now one car lighter, kept on going.

Bhodi slid over, seeking handholds on what was now the end car. He didn't know how much ground the soldiers had covered, but whatever it was, it would be too much. He wasn't going to have time to go to every single car and pick off every single lock.

Then another desperate idea occurred to him. Boy, a

few more of these, he thought, and he could become the strategist of the crew, instead of the hotshot marksman. But it was his uncanny aim that was going to be needed now.

He edged around the side of the car and could see all the way down to the front. Out of the corner of his eye he saw the soldiers making their way along the top of the train. But he also saw exactly what he thought he would. All the padlocks were exactly on the same place on all the cars—about waist high for someone standing inside the car. Trust German efficiency.

He took aim and fired. The Phaser beam lanced out and sliced straight down, splitting open all the locks all the way down the length of the train. A moment later the train rounded a curve and Bhodi breathed a sigh of relief. He would never have been able to make a shot like that unless the train were absolutely straight.

Some sixth sense warned Bhodi and he looked up, at the same time bringing his Phaser to bear. There was a soldier directly overhead, taking aim with his pistol. Bhodi fired, knocking the pistol out of the soldier's hand. The soldier was so startled that he lost his balance and tumbled right past Bhodi to the ground. Quickly Bhodi scrambled up to the roof and dropped to his belly.

He saw them approaching, the closest of them only three cars away. There were four of them in all. Bhodi started to fire, placing shots just to the right and left of them, taking care not to hit any of them directly with the beam. They dodged frantically, realizing the deadly potential of the ray.

Bhodi strained his eyes, the eye shield of his helmet protecting his face from the high wind. Coming up about a half mile down was a grove of tall trees. The branches, however, didn't hang nearly low enough to be a threat, even to people waltzing around on the top of a train. But that was something Bhodi intended to do something about.

Carefully placing his shots Bhodi opened fire on the trees

in the distance. Not realizing that he was no longer aiming at them, the soldiers continued to duck while trying to inch their way forward.

Upper branches started to crash down into lower branches, and at one point a huge clump of leaves and branches was hanging down at just the right height. As the train engine rolled past the branches, they didn't so much as scrape the roof.

But when the cars with the crouching Nazis came to the branches, the outcome became evident. Like a giant fly swatter the low-hanging branches started to knock the Nazis off the train, one by one. It happened so quickly that by the time the last of the Nazis caught on to what was happening, he too had been swept off the top of the train by the well-placed (depending on your point of view) branches.

"All right!" crowed Bhodi. "Clean sweep!"

Abandoning all subterfuge now, Bhodi ran as fast as he could along the roof of the train, leaping with agility from one car to the next. As he did, he kept on shouting, "Get ready to slide open the doors when the train stops! Get ready to go, the locks are busted off. Get ready!"

He paused for only a moment to glance back, but Gretta's car was long out of sight. He only hoped that he had managed to put enough distance between Gretta's car and the caboose that had held the soldiers. But he couldn't worry about every aspect. He had to do the best that he could do.

He was only one car away from the engine now and then suddenly he saw it. The tunnel. Coming up fast.

There was still time. He didn't know what was on the other side of the tunnel—for all he knew they would suddenly find themselves on the steep side of a mountain, with nowhere for the refugees to run to. Here the ground was still flat.

"Let's do it," said Bhodi under his breath. Taking a breath he vaulted from one end of the car to the other so that he was now directly behind, and looking down on, the engine. His Phaser out, his aim sure, his Phaser beam flashed out and sliced through the couplings that held the rest of the train to the engine.

It cut through effortlessly. The steel might as well have been cardboard, and in less time than it takes to tell, the locomotive came loose from the unholy cargo it was transporting.

Bhodi let out a triumphant yell as the car that he was standing on started to slow down.

And then he saw the danger—one more soldier, hanging out of a side window of the engine cab. Aiming dead on at Bhodi.

Even as he saw the soldier, Bhodi prepared to leap backward, but his reaction was too slow because the soldier was already squeezing the trigger of his luger.

It was an extremely difficult shot. Pistols from a distance are not always accurate, and a shot from one moving object at another, both at different rates of speed, should have been flat out impossible to make.

Either the soldier was an incredible marksman or just very very lucky . . . Bhodi never knew which. All he knew was that a moment before he actually heard the "crack" of the bullet, he felt something like a sledgehammer smash against the side of his helmet.

It didn't penetrate. His armor and helmet were not of Earth and could withstand the bullet impact. Nevertheless Bhodi Li was staggered, his head ringing, his vision swimming before him. The entire landscape tilted wildly. Madly he waved his arms, trying to regain his balance, and he almost managed it.

But he had forgotten about the tunnel. Even at the slower speed the cars had continued to approach the tunnel, carved into the side of a looming mountain. Bhodi managed to refocus a split second before he slammed into the side of the mountain.

With a yell Bhodi toppled off the train. He fell to the

left, landing with a bone-crunching thud on the ground at the mouth of the tunnel. The train continued to roll a few feet and then ground to a halt.

Bhodi coughed and his chest hurt. He hoped he hadn't busted a rib. To his right the people in the cars were already shoving the doors open. Bhodi was appalled to see that many of them were afraid to leave the car, as if this were all some sort of setup. Then they started to run out of the cars, first a few and then dozens, and then the area was filled with hundreds and hundreds of people running. Running for their lives.

Several started towards Bhodi. Even though he was fighting to remain conscious, he frantically waved them off. "Don't worry about me!" he shouted. "I'm fine. Get going! Get going. You haven't got much time."

There were rifle shots, and Bhodi started to get to his feet. Then the world started to spin around him and he doubled over, unable to get his bearings.

"Run!" he screamed, and then from behind him a rifle butt was brought down on the back of his head like a club.

He fell flat on his stomach. He looked up at a soldier standing over him, rifle pointed at his head.

Bhodi grinned lopsidedly and croaked out, "Awww. Did I mess things up for you? I'm soooo sorry."

The soldier brought his foot back and then swiftly towards Bhodi's face. Then everything went black.

13
Aftermath

The first thing he heard was water drippping.

The first thing he saw was nothing.

The first thing he smelled was . . . well, it was unpleasant.

He went back to seeing, or trying to. Slowly he opened his eyes and was dismayed to discover that it was still just as dark as before. Then slowly, ever so slowly, his eyes grew accustomed to his darkened surroundings.

He was lying flat on the floor of a cell. It was made of concrete and the first thing he managed to make out was a rat scuttling by him. They ignored each other and slowly Bhodi worked on sitting up.

It took him a while. If he moved too quickly, he felt a pounding in his skull that made him think his entire head would just roll off his shoulders. He put his hand to his head and realized that his helmet was gone. As he dropped his arm back to the floor, he heard a chain rattling and wondered where it was coming from. Then he realized . . . it was coming from him.

He slowly raised his hand in front of his face and stared

at the length of chain dangling from a manacle around his wrist. He pulled on the manacle, but it was made of solid iron and didn't show the least bit of interest in being ripped off. Slowly he turned, following the trail of the chain. It was attached to the wall, affixed to a bolt in the wall about the size of Rhode Island. There was a second length of chain attached to the bolt as well, and Bhodi discovered that the chain was attached to his left leg. He gave the chain an experimental pull but it just laughed at his efforts.

He stood up slowly, his full concentration being given to not falling over again. "So far so good," he muttered. He patted himself down. His belt and power plate and, naturally, his Phaser, were all gone.

"Swell," he said. "Just terrific." He forced himself not to dwell on the hopelessness of his situation. He started to inspect his cell, but what he found wasn't heartening. It wasn't much bigger than his bedroom at home. There was no window in the cell itself, except for a small one set in the door. Way too small for him to fit through.

He walked over to the door and discovered that the chains would only let him get halfway there. He shook his head. This was not going well . . . not well at all.

He sat down to wait and see what would happen.

He didn't have to wait very long.

For an hour he listened to the sounds of marching feet constantly going past his door, but eventually one pair stopped directly in front of it.

Someone he didn't recognize . . . a soldier, he imagined . . . peered through the window at him. Bhodi, seated at the far end of the cell on the floor, gave a cheery little wave. The soldier's face withdrew from the window, and then he heard the sound of a large lock being manipulated.

The door swung wide, and Bhodi's heart sank as he saw who entered.

"Well, matey," growled Pirarr. "I understand you've been giving the authorities a few problems."

Mandarr, standing directly behind him, laughed deep in his throat. Destructarr's face was unreadable.

Around his shoulders Pirarr wore a replica of a snake, its fanged head hissing over his right shoulder. Pirarr stroked it absently as if it were a pet. "You tried to spring some prisoners, so we've been told."

"It was a nice try, boy," Mandarr said, sneering. "But from what we've been told, most of the people you so nobly set free have already been caught again. And the rest are certain to be apprehended within no time at all."

With a growl, Destructarr said, "So you see, all your work was for nothing."

Bhodi looked from one to the other of them, and then, defiantly, he smiled.

"What are you grinning about?" demanded Pirarr.

"I'm just picturing what the Warlord will do when I send you back to him," said Bhodi. "Just as I always do. Just as I always will."

"Not this time," said Mandarr. "You're not going to win." He pulled out his Phaser and aimed it right at Bhodi's face. "I could kill you right now."

"Go ahead," Bhodi dared him.

A look of pure fury filled Mandarr's face, but then Pirarr put a hand on the end of Mandarr's weapon and forced him to lower it. "None of that, matey," he said sternly. "We've already come up with a plan. Let's stick to it."

"And what might that plan be?" asked Bhodi, acting as if he didn't care.

Pirarr stared at him. "Oh, I think it would be of particular interest to you, Bhodi Li, seeing as how it's going to be very pertinent to you." He chucked a large thumb in Mandarr's direction. "Mandarr was a lot like you once. A young hotshot. But we made him the way he is. We think he's a lot more useful that way."

He leaned forward and thrust his grizzled, green face

into Bhodi's. "So we're going to take you back to Arr with us. We're going to make you like Mandarr here."

Although he felt inner revulsion, Bhodi remained cool. "You can just forget that."

Mandarr leaned forward now as well. "No. You can remember it. You can remember it as you sit here in this dark, dank cell, while we aid this gentleman here in winning his little war."

Bhodi looked up and his heart froze.

He had only seen pictures of him, pictures of the odd man with the Charlie Chaplin moustache.

Now Adolf Hitler stood in the doorway of his cell, staring at him with undisguised hatred and . . .

And what? Could that be fear in his eyes?

Bhodi suddenly lurched forward and yelled, "Boo!"

Hitler jumped back immediately, and several of his personal guards ran in front of him to protect him from potential attack.

Bhodi sat back and laughed. "You want to hear a song? My grandfather taught it to me." And he sang out, "When der Fuehrer says, 'We is the master race,' we Sig Heil," and he blew a rude Bronx cheer, "Heil," cheered again, "right in der Fuehrer's face."

With quick steps Hitler walked forward, swung his hand back and slapped Bhodi across the cheek. It stung a little, but not as much as his words had stung Hitler, he knew. His granddad would be so proud of him. He wondered bleakly if he'd ever see him again.

"I'll kill you myself," said Hitler, and started to pull out his gun.

"Now-now . . . let's not be hasty, mein Fuehrer," said Pirarr quickly. "You'll bring bad luck, worse than you know, down on top of yourself if you kill this one. Take my word for it."

Hitler turned his malevolent gaze on Pirarr, looked back at Bhodi, then holstered his gun.

"Now," said Mandarr, "I'm afraid we're going to have

to let you stew here for a few days, Bhodi. You see, we're going to be quite busy thwarting an allied attack on June 6.''

Bhodi's eyes widened. There *was* something happening in early June, 1944. June 6. But . . . but what was it? He strained to remember. His grandfather's voice sounded faintly in his head, but he couldn't recall what was being said. What happened? Where? It was something really huge, but what?

''As I said, we'll be quite occupied,'' said Mandarr. ''But don't think we're going to forget about you. We'll be back . . . after we complete our little job.''

Hitler spoke then to Mandarr in curt, brittle tones. ''We shall speak of this again . . . this going off on your own.''

Mandarr sighed, obviously trying to control himself as he turned to Hitler. ''Now, mein Fuehrer, we've spoken of this already, a number of times. We want to make very clear to you just how much you're going to need us. If we tell you where the allied invasion will take place, you'll be there with all the troops you can muster. Our fighting strength will be superfluous.''

''It's Calais,'' said Hitler. ''The allies will be attacking at Calais. We've picked up allied radio transmissions that state this. This subterfuge of yours is pointless.''

Mandarr placed his hands on his hips. ''I wouldn't even try to contradict you, mein Fuehrer,'' he said silkily. ''Nevertheless, you respect our weapons and powers. I submit that you should respect our arrangement as well. An airplane and pilot to take us where we wish to go, no questions asked. And you may just be in for a few surprises.''

Hitler frowned. ''You are supernatural. I don't trust that which is supernatural, even though I want to harness its power to my will. I don't wish to be overanxious . . . after all, I still remember that debacle with the Ark of the Covenant a few years back. So I will accede to your requests . . . for now. The boy lives. You may have the latitude you need. But I warn you"—and he raised a finger—"do not seek to betray me. Or despite all your power I will have you wiped from the face of the planet."

"That's usually my job," said Bhodi.

They all looked at him, and Bhodi suddenly started to sing again, "To not love the Fuehrer is a great disgrace, so we . . ." But before he could get to the rude sounds again, Hitler had turned on his heel and started for the door. "Hey, wait! Don't you want to hear how the rest of the song goes?" But Hitler was out the door and gone.

"You upset him, Bhodi Li. That wasn't very nice." Mandarr grabbed Bhodi's face in one hand and squeezed until Bhodi thought his jaw would snap. Then Mandarr hurled him against the far wall, where he landed in a heap.

"Think about this, while you're rotting in your cell," said Mandarr. "We're going to be there, wiping out all the allied forces. All of them. What was considered the greatest sea and land victory in the history of armed warfare is going to become the greatest defeat the allies will ever know as we kill every single soldier."

Bhodi forced himself to sound casual. "And just where is this going to be?"

Mandarr stared at him incredulously. "You don't know? You don't remember? Ah, Bhodi Li . . . you should learn your history better, and more often."

"Oh, I remember now," said Bhodi quickly. "But I bet you don't."

Mandarr laughed. "Then you would lose your bet. Don't worry, Bhodi. We'll be back. I'll be sure to tell you about the slaughter in every . . . single . . . detail." He savored the last words and laughed raucously. Then he turned, and he, Pirarr and Destructarr left Bhodi's cell.

"Wait!" shouted Bhodi, but the only answer he received was a door being slammed shut. It echoed through the cell.

With a sigh Bhodi sagged against the wall. He had

really screwed things up this time. Thus far the three Dark
Guardians had accomplished everything they'd set out to
do, while he had gone off on a complete tangent. He had
acted with his heart rather than listening to MOM's instructions. If Leon had been there, Leon would have given
him a swift shot in the side of the head. Actually, probably
not, for Leon was soft-hearted despite his fearsome appearance. But he would have reamed him up one side and
down the other, and rightly so.

And then, something horrible occurred to Bhodi. Mandarr
had been talking about wiping out the troops entirely, to
the man.

But Bhodi's grandpa Lou had spoken frequently of being
part of some major offensive during the war. What if it
was this one?

What if the Dark Guardians killed Bhodi's grandfather?
Grandpa Lou had not yet met his grandmother. If that was
the case, then not only would thousands upon thousands of
men die tragically at the hands of the Dark Guardians, but
also Bhodi Li would never be born!

What would happen to him, he wondered? Would he
fade out of existence slowly? Would he just vanish like a
soap bubble? Would Parcival and Tivia even remember
him?

He stared down at a rat that was staring back up at him
with a questioning gaze. Maybe Tivia wouldn't even remember him . . . that was a depressing thought.

And he said to the rat, "So we Heil, razz, Heil, razz,
right in der Fuehrer's face."

14

Assault and Battery

Day had passed into night and into the following day.

It had been many hours now since Parcival and Tivia had lost track of their teammate. Many hours that Tivia had spent waxing at length about Bhodi Li. What she said alternated, depending upon her mood. About half the time she spent being openly concerned about Bhodi's welfare. Where was he? Was he alive? Why hadn't he come back?

The rest of the time she fumed about how he had left them in the lurch. How he had acted recklessly, and not for the first time. He had jeopardized an already dangerous mission, and if he was alive, she'd probably kill him.

Parcival, in the meantime, sat on the floor of Gretta's living room. After much digging around, he had discovered exactly what he thought he would discover—a short-wave radio hidden behind a panel in the basement. Gretta, ever cautious, had not even told the Photon Guardians about the mechanism. Using the equipment Parcival had tried to broadcast to whomever Gretta spoke to, to inform them of how the entire operation had fallen apart and that they should do whatever they could to rescue Gretta. But he had been unable to get any sort of response. He could only assume that if someone was listening, they were waiting for him to give some sort of identifying code name, which he obviously did not have. Finally he just transmitted blindly, hoping that someone was there, although he said nothing to give away his own whereabouts. Just in the event someone was listening who shouldn't be.

Once he'd done his transmitting, he'd started to disassemble the entire transmitter. Tivia had watched with fascination as he had taken a small clock and removed the gears and works and then proceeded to reassemble it. Except he was using the pieces from the transmitter to do so. The only part that Tivia saw him put back on was one of the clock hands, which now hung limply on the face.

He had put aside the entire mechanism for several hours during the night to get some sleep. During that time Tivia had remained awake and watchful, alert for any soldiers or men from the Gestapo who might return to Gretta's house now and disturb the Photon Warriors in their work. No one did, though, and now it was Tivia's turn to get some sleep as Parcival returned diligently to his labors.

Her sleep was not restful. She saw Bhodi, and to her relief he was not dead. He seemed to be locked away somewhere, looking sad and miserable. She wanted to take him in her arms, he looked so pathetic, and then she would . . .

Then her mother's scowling face appeared in front of her. "Remember who you are, Tivia," she said sternly. "Remember our society. He is not for you, Tivia. No man is for you. You must remain pure in the ways of the Warrior."

"Yes, Mother," she replied, "I know what you say. But he makes me feel . . . I don't know . . ."

"But I do know. Beware these feelings, Tivia. It's a

trap, to weaken our spirits. Men are suspicious and distrustful of women who are stronger than they are. They always want to introduce confusion into you so that you will be less powerful . . . ideally less powerful than they are. That must not happen to you, Tivia. You are a princess and vital to us.''

''But Mother . . .''

She sounded understanding. ''It is natural for you to have some feelings for Bhodi Li. You have worked closely with him in many life and death situations. Developing an attachment is natural, but you must remain at a distance. Otherwise,'' she said sternly, ''you cannot remain as a Photon Warrior.''

Tivia was staggered. ''But, Mother, it's my responsibility—''

''Your responsibility is what I tell you, Tivia.'' The dream image of her mother strode towards her. ''I permitted you to become a Photon Guardian because you were needed. But I did so with a certain amount of trepidation, for I was concerned that just this might happen. If your attachment to Bhodi Li grows beyond simple camaraderie, you must leave the Photon Guardians. And you will never see Bhodi Li again.''

''You can't do that!''

Her mother stepped forward and, placing both hands on her daughter's shoulders, started to shake her. ''I can and I will. Remember who you are. You're Tivia, the princess. Tivia, Tivia . . .''

And then, slowly, her mother's voice started to turn into Parcival's.

''Tivia,'' and again, ''Tivia.''

She woke up instantly. She never woke up gradually, slowly becoming resigned to another morning. She always came to full wakefulness immediately. It was a very handy ability to have in case an enemy was sneaking up on you while you slept.

Parcival was shaking her now, saying, ''I'd let you keep

sleeping, but I've finished the tracking device. We can go after Bhodi now.''

She blinked. Why did Parcival look so odd? Even as the question framed itself, she recalled the answer. He still had that makeup on, as did she. They'd have to reapply it before they went out again.

"Parcival, you're remarkable."

"I know," he said matter of factly.

"So where precisely is Bhodi?" She sat up, rubbing the last vestiges of sleep from her eyes.

Parcival held up the clock. He had removed the plug from the end of the wire and hotwired it directly to the small computer mechanism on his wrist. "I don't know exactly where yet. But I do know what direction he's in."

Tivia stared at the clock. The single hand on the clock face was pointing at the three.

"He's due east," said Parcival. "It's working perfectly, homing in on the instantaneous translator in Bhodi's ear. Since the translator was based on my design, it was child's play to figure out how to tap into it."

"But why isn't it homing in on ours?" asked Tivia. "How does it know which one to look for?"

"Easy," said Parcival. "I designed it to ignore any translator device within a five-foot radius. Once we get within five feet of Bhodi Li, it will stop working altogether. Until then, it'll take us right to him."

Tivia clenched a fist. "Great. Let's go and bail Bhodi out of whatever he's gotten himself into."

After reapplying the makeup, Parcival and Tivia set out. They were extremely fortunate in that the trip across the city was largely uneventful. Several times marching feet alerted them to yet another squad of goose-stepping soldiers heading their way. Every time they would promptly seek a hiding place, not wanting to fall into the hands of the Germans or, just as bad, waste time in a pointless firefight in the streets of Berlin.

Parcival consulted his tracer frequently, pulling it out from under his large coat to see if the hand had changed direction. It guided them straight and true through Berlin, on their mission to find their missing teammate.

After more than an hour of steady tracking, they stopped in front of a low-slung, ugly-looking building. Parcival consulted his tracker and nodded. "He's in there. I'd bet on it."

Tivia nodded. "All right. I'm going in. You wait here."

"No way!" said Parcival. "I'm a Photon Guardian too."

"I know that," was the patient reply. "But your Phaser was part of your computer rig, and that's destroyed."

Parcival opened his coat. His Phaser was tucked into the belt. His bat was slung through his vest. "I disconnected it. You think I'm going into a fight unarmed? True, I'm not a marksman like Bhodi, or a hand-to-hand expert like you. But I'll pull my own weight, don't you worry."

Tivia nodded briskly. "All right. You've convinced me. But we're going to have to be as silent as possible about this. No telling how many of our enemies are in there. The further we can get in quietly, the better off we'll be."

Tivia left her Phaser in its holster, but in one palm she held a half dozen star blades and in the other hand were her nunchuks—two staves a foot long connected by a small length of chain. Deadly weapons in the right hands, and Tivia's were most definitely the right hands.

There were two guards standing on either side of the front door, so Tivia and Parcival elected to walk around the block and try for a rear assault.

There were bars over the windows—clearly this was a place that would be both tough to get into and even tougher getting out of. The two Photon Guardians walked around the block to the back of the building, looking as casual as they could. There were no windows at street level—the only ones were on the second floor and, naturally, they had those blasted bars blocking the way.

Tivia turned to Parcival and said in a low voice, "Do you see anyone coming?"

"No."

"Good. Watch my back."

Before he could say another word, Tivia crouched and then leaped upward, snagging onto the bars of one of the windows. She crouched there on the wall like a spider and peered through the window.

It was a conference room of some sort, empty now. On the wall was a large map of an area that she didn't recognize. That was hardly surprising. Being from an alien planet, Earth geography was hardly her strong suit.

No time to waste. She slid the five star blades, wrapped in cloth similar to the mesh she wore, into her coat pocket. Then she placed the razorsharp blades of the sixth one against the first of the four bars on the window that blocked her way.

It sliced right through. She smiled under her mask. No shoddy Earth metal could stand up to good old Nivian workwomanship. Within seconds she had cut through all the bars, top and bottom, and she gathered them up in her hand.

She slid through the now unbarred window without making a sound, then turned and look down. Parcival was standing watch on the street below, and when she hissed his name, he looked up and blinked in surprise. She leaned out the window, extending a hand. Parcival gathered all his strength and leaped toward her.

Although his own abilities were augmented by the power of Photon, he was still not as strong or agile as Tivia. As a result his leap brought him up short of his objective, namely the window. But before he could fall back to the ground, Tivia reached out, her hand snagging his upper arm. As if he weighed nothing, Tivia hauled him into the room with her.

"Thanks," he whispered. She nodded, then picked up the four bars that now lay on the floor. She hefted them experimentally and nodded.

"These could be useful," she said, and handed him two.

He took them, nodding his thanks. Then he consulted his tracker, getting down to business. "This way," he said. "And let's hope we don't get spotted."

They opened the door and there were four soldiers lounging in the hallway. They looked at Tivia and Parcival in disbelief.

"So much for that hope," muttered Parcival.

Before Parcival could even move, however, Tivia was on them. Parcival was stunned at her fierceness. He had never seen her move that quickly before, nor could he recall her being quite so deadly. Even as a front snapkick incapacitated one guard, Tivia was whirling the nunchuks above her head. She brained a second, then a third. The fourth backed away from her, pulling his pistol as he did so. But he backed towards Parcival, who leaped high in the air and brought the iron bar down as hard as he could on the soldier's head. It rang like a bell off the helmet but left a huge dent. It also left the guard dizzy enough for Tivia to finish him off.

They didn't waste time congratulating themselves. Tivia threw open a door that she believed to be the room they'd just come out of. However she had gotten slightly turned around in the fight and she opened the wrong one.

She gasped. "Parcival. Look at this."

It was a small weapons room. There were guns, grenades, ammo—

And over in one corner, a red helmet, a power pack, belt, and a Photon Phaser.

Tivia was suddenly saddened beyond understanding. Bhodi's gear looked so empty separated from Bhodi himself. It was as if something vital, a piece of him, had been removed and stashed in another room.

Tivia gathered it up, found a backpack and stuffed in the Phaser, belt and power pack. The helmet was too large, so she placed it on her own head. She tapped the plastic shield that now protected her face and shrugged.

Parcival was studying the grenades and now removed several from a box and placed them in his coat pockets. "All right. Let's go."

"Which way?"

He stared at the tracer but wasn't certain which way it was pointing. Then he realized that he was holding it on a horizontal plane. On a hunch he held it vertically and immediately the hand snapped into a definite downward direction.

"He's downstairs," said Parcival.

They headed down the hallway, got to the stairs and started down when they came upon another group of soldiers. Tivia took a step forward but Parcival said, "No!" and hurled a grenade at the guards. It exploded the moment it reached their midst, gas billowing out and enveloping them. Tivia and Parcival, of one mind, took a deep breath and leaped over the soldiers' heads. Somersaulting they landed on the bottom step of the stairway, now on the first floor.

Guards came running, seemingly from all sides. With a loud battle cry Tivia started hurling star blades. The deadly little devices knocked rifles out of their hands and Tivia's nunchuks knocked the thoughts out of their heads.

They fought their way into the main foyer. They were at such close quarters that none of the soldiers dared shoot for fear of hitting each other. They tried to lay hands on Tivia, to bring her down by force of numbers, but she was too agile. Whenever they pressed too hard, Tivia would leap over their heads and pummel them into senselessness on her way down.

Parcival hurled another gas grenade behind them. Soldiers banged into each other, unable to see, coughing and hacking. Parcival at one point almost forgot to hold his breath and took in a bit of the gas himself. He coughed furiously, his eyes tearing, and for a moment he couldn't see which way they were supposed to go.

Tivia and Parcival retreated into the lobby, which was illuminated by an immense chandelier. Parcival cast a quick glance at a painting of Adolf Hitler and muttered to himself, "The guy's everywhere." Then he glanced up and saw the chandelier.

"Tivia, quick! This way."

Tivia knocked two more unconscious with the whirring nunchuks, throttled a third with them and then hurled him at his fellows. She followed Parcival and they backed up to a far end of the lobby.

"Parcival, if you have some bright idea, use it now," said Tivia. Several dozen soldiers, the survivors of the first assault, bore down on them, rifles out.

Parcival had his Phaser in hand and now he aimed upward and fired once. The shot took out the chandelier support and the huge lamp, with a resounding tinkling of glass, fell on top of the soldiers.

They went down beneath the sheer weight, and in no time at all Tivia and Parcival were upon them. Imprisoned beneath the chandelier as they were, the soldiers could not resist at all. Within minutes they had all been clubbed into unconsciousness.

Tivia stood back and surveyed the mess. "The two of us against over three dozen men."

"They never had a chance," sniffed Parcival. He consulted his tracer. "Down again."

They found another stairway downwards into the basement and there discovered a row of doors. Each door had a small window set into it at eye level. A string of lightbulbs lit the corridor dimly.

Parcival, in the lead, ran as fast as he could, with Tivia right behind him. After a couple of moments, the tracer suddenly seemed to go dead. Parcival stopped so suddenly that Tivia almost ran him down.

He pointed wordlessly to a door. Tivia understood the need for caution. In theory Bhodi was in there, but for all they knew someone else might be in there, too.

The only thing they had going for them was the element of surprise. In order to maintain that surprise they would have to make an abrupt entrance into the cell. Calling out Bhodi's name would just alert whoever was in there. Hopefully this was a needless caution, but needless caution was better than no caution when it was needed.

Tivia took a star blade and hurled it at the lock. It shattered the lock easily and the next instant Tivia and Parcival leaped into the cell, Phasers drawn.

It was so dark that Tivia couldn't see anything and then, within the next second, something wrapped itself around her throat.

15

Only Mandarr and Englishmen Go Out in the Noonday Sun

For several hours Bhodi Li sat in his cell, steaming over the chain of events. Finally he decided that he wasn't going to just sit around and take it anymore. He was going to take control of the situation, break out, find his companions and then go beat the crap out of Mandarr and his cronies.

The problem was getting beyond the first part, namely getting free.

With that goal foremost on his mind, Bhodi turned his attention to the little matter of the chains that had him as a mere extension of a prison wall. He began to pull, exerting his full Photon strength, on the chains that had him anchored. In his left hand he held the chain that was attached to his left hand. In his other hand he held the chain that was attached to his left foot.

Hour after hour the pattern was the same. He would pull, strain with all his might on the unyielding iron chains. At some point he always thought there was some give to it, but the chains continued to resist his greatest endeavors.

"Bhodi Li, big Photon Warrior," they seemed to taunt him. "Inside you're just little Christopher Jarvis, who's only happy when he's playing shoot-'em-up in the Photon arena. Give it up, Jarvis. Fighting monsters from space is fine, but now you've got good, old, down-to-earth iron to deal with, and you can't hack it."

Bhodi doubled and redoubled his efforts. He dug his feet in and pulled and pulled, his teeth set, his eyes closed. He pulled again, and the muscles on his arms stood out, the vein on his forehead pulsed and throbbed blue against his skin, which was becoming red from the exertion.

He pictured his grandfather being cut down by Mandarr, and he pulled and strained.

He saw Gretta running for her life, shots being fired behind her, and he yanked harder still, refusing to give in to the agony that ripped through him.

He heard something. At first he thought it was his own back snapping under the strain even as he dug in his heels and gave yet another huge pull.

There was a sound like the crack of a bullet, and then Bhodi fell backwards. Back several feet, beyond where the chain had been permitting him to go. He sat there for a moment, dazed, and then pulled on the chain experimentally. It was completely slack. He kept pulling and heard something rattling across the floor, a heavy object being dragged.

He pulled it all the way to him and held it up. It was the

anchor and bracket which had previously been attached to the wall. The chain had held up under his exertions, but the wall itself had given way. He had managed to rip the brackets right out of the wall.

He grinned as he went over to the wall to find a gaping hole where the bracket had been. Now there was solid dirt and mud, some already falling in the cell. What a crying shame. If he'd been on an upper floor he would have a direct hole to the outside. But since he was in the basement, all he had was dirt. Bhodi pondered. Perhaps he could tunnel his way out.

All during his struggles he had been trying to dredge up everything he could remember about World War II. It was annoying that thus far all he could recall were meaningless trivialities. Nothing truly important.

Then a name and address leaped to him, a bolt from the blue.

Winston Churchill. 10 Downing Street. Grandpa Lou had spoken highly of Churchill many a time, talking about his wit and regaling Chris with well-known anecdotes. Churchill was a big shot in the war somehow, and he lived at 10 Downing Street.

Great. Now where the heck was 10 Downing Street? He didn't know why, but he thought it was England.

Maybe Churchill could help him, if he could get there. Churchill could tell him where this big offensive was supposed to be, and the three Photon Warriors could head there and take the Dark Guardians out.

Good plan. Now how to get to Churchill? And how did he find Tivia and Parcival, for single-handedly he didn't have a prayer against Mandarr and his cronies.

Suddenly, from overhead, there was a tremendous crash. Bhodi wondered what the devil it was.

Then, moments later, his sharp hearing picked up footsteps headed down the hallway outside his cell door. He realized that if guards came in and found him unchained, they would just try to find some new and even stronger way to imprison him. And he had no more time to remain a guest of Uncle Adolf and friends.

Bhodi, picking up the dragging end of the chains, hid himself in the darkness a few feet to the side of the door. Moments later he heard someone at the lock. They were coming into his cell! This was when he would break free.

A dark form entered his cell and immediately Bhodi hurled the chain at the intruder. It wrapped around the intruder's neck and Bhodi yanked his prisoner toward himself.

But before he could get a grip on his catch, Bhodi's prisoner slammed the base of a hand up against Bhodi's mouth. Bhodi went down, moaning.

The dark figure stood there for a moment and then said, "Bhodi? Is that you?"

Bhodi looked up and squinted in the darkness. "Tivia?"

Her faintly mocking voice floated to him from the dimness. "Well, well, well, if it isn't the wayward Photon Guardian," she said, pulling the chain off herself.

"I didn't recognize you with that helmet on. Hey! That's mine!"

From behind her came Parcival. "We found him?"

"More like we found each other," said Bhodi, getting to his feet and rubbing his chin ruefully. "Boy, Tivia, you pack a punch."

"I had been trying to decide when we found you whether or not I should be glad to see you or slug you. I guess fate made its choice."

"Sure did. Let's get out of here."

Using her star blades, Tivia sliced the manacles off him. Then she unslung the backpack and pulled out Bhodi's equipment. As he strapped it on, she removed the helmet and handed that back to him as well. With a nod of thanks he put that on and hefted his Phaser affectionately. Within moments he was back in his full rig.

"Okay, which way?"

"The way we came," said Parcival.

"But won't there be soldiers and guys like that?" asked Bhodi.

"Oh, yes," said Parcival. "But I wouldn't be concerned about them if I were you."

As they headed upstairs Bhodi quickly filled them in on what had happened, glossing over the entire incident with the train and focusing on the encounter with Pirarr, Mandarr, Destructarr . . .

"And Hitlarr," he added ruefully. "That guy really gave me the creeps."

They got to the upstairs foyer and Bhodi whistled in appreciation. "I'll say this for you guys. You are thorough. Where now?"

"Out the front door," said Parcival with a shrug. "Why not?"

"Why not indeed?" said Tivia. They went to the front door, opened it . . .

And saw what appeared to be an entire battalion of soldiers running toward them.

Bhodi slammed the door shut, shoved his back against it and said, "That's why not."

They bolted towards the upstairs. As they did, they heard gunfire and bullets start to slam against the door, several of them penetrating. "This is just not my day," said Bhodi as they ran up the stairs three at a time.

At the top of the stairs they paused, trying to figure out what to do. At that moment the soldiers crashed through the door. It exploded inward from the impact, shards of wood flying.

"C'mon, let's move it!" snapped Bhodi, and they ran down the corridor of the second floor. Instinctively Tivia ran into the room through which she had made her initial entry. One of the four soldiers she had dumped in there was just starting to come around. Without hesitation she kicked him in the head and he fell back unconscious.

Tivia went to the window and immediately ducked back as a bullet whizzed through. "I think we'd better stay away from the window," she noted drily.

Bhodi was barely paying attention. He was staring hard at the map on the wall and suddenly he snapped his fingers. "Perfect! This is perfect. It's a map of Europe. And here's England. England is where Churchill is."

"That's real nice, Bhodi," said Parcival, lobbing a gas grenade out the window. "But unfortunately Germany is where *we* are. And who knows where the transportation device is . . ."

Bhodi reached into one of the cylinders in his belt, opened it, and extracted the device. "Yo."

Parcival turned, wide-eyed. Even Tivia looked stunned. "I'd assumed they'd taken it off you."

"Nah. I stashed it in the belt after I used it the second time."

"You've just mentioned the main problem, Bhodi," said Parcival. "You've used it twice. One more time and it's out of power completely."

Bhodi nodded briskly. "Then we've got to do it right the first time."

There was another shot and it embedded itself in the wall just to the right of Tivia's head. She tossed off a random shot with her Phaser just to scare the soldiers on the ground back. She was tempted to chew Bhodi out for bringing them to the point where they were down to one transport and had accomplished almost nothing except getting themselves imprisoned, shot at and (maybe) killed. But that would serve no purpose. There was never any point to placing blame. That didn't solve problems. Only action did.

"Some action, fellows," she said. "The longer we stay here the more hazardous things get."

Bhodi was studying the map. He had found England, but was having trouble locating Downing Street, where

Churchill was. Then, suddenly, he saw a spot on the map
that had been marked with a little red circle. He cast an
eye along the street name and discovered that it was indeed
Downing Street. Chances were extremely good that this
little spot was Number 10. It would figure that the Germans would have marked the headquarters of one of their
greatest nuisances.

"Parcival," he called, and the boy genius was at his
side. "This point here—can you set the transporter for
these coordinates?"

Parcival looked at him with an "Are you implying that I
can't?" expression. With an expert eye he figured out the
longitude and latitude. He quickly readjusted the numbers
configuration on the transporter device, then turned to
Bhodi and said, "Got it. But you'd better be right about
this, Bhodi."

"I will be," said Bhodi. "Tivia! We're out of here."

Doubled over to avoid being shot, Tivia scooted across
the room and stood at their side.

"Stay close now," said Parcival. He gave it one half
twist and immediately a cocoon of blue light surrounded
them. Just as they dematerialized a bullet passed right
through where Bhodi had been.

Once again Bhodi felt himself being turned inside out,
and that bizarre momentary disorientation that always accompanied having his molecules scrambled and sent
who-knew-where.

He landed with a thud and knew that the very last of the
cylinder's energy had been tapped out making this final
jump.

Before his vision had even cleared though, he heard
yells of shock. At the same time that he recognized those
yells not to be from Parcival and Tivia, he also heard the
sounds of hammers being cocked.

He looked around slowly.

He was eye to eye with a balding man who looked to be in about his late sixties. He had a cigar clenched between his teeth and a look of pure astonishment on his face. His suit was grey and wrinkled, as if he'd been sleeping in it recently. He wore a bow tie, but a real one. Not like one of those cheap clip-on things that his folks had made Bhodi wear when he was a little kid.

Bhodi stared at the man and heard more hammers being pulled back. Behind the map on the wall was a map similar to what he had seen, and for one wild moment he thought that maybe they were still back in Berlin. But then he realized that such was not the case.

Slowly, very slowly, he looked around. He and Tivia and Parcival were all back to back, forming a little triangle. They were in a large room, surrounded by men who had clearly been in the middle of a lot of work. There were papers spread all over, charts that Bhodi only caught a glimpse of.

Four men, obviously high-ranking army officers by the jackets they wore, already had guns out and had trained them on the Photon Guardians. One of them shouted, "Kalish! Get your men in here, now!" He had a crisp British accent.

"Now, that won't be necessary," began Bhodi, but before he could get any further, British soldiers had filled the room. They were all clearly stunned at the bizarrely-garbed intruders wearing futuristic clothing underneath somewhat frumpy raincoats. Except for one whom they assumed to be the leader.

The officer who had summoned the soldiers stepped forward and held his gun directly in Bhodi's face. To the balding man next to him he said, "Perhaps you'd best leave for your own safety, Mr. Prime Minister."

Realization came to Bhodi as he turned quickly and said, "Prime Minister? You're Churchill, aren't you?"

"Now, see here, young man, don't be impertinent,"

said the officer, his gun never wavering. "Mr. Prime Minister, please— "

Churchill took a deep drag on his cigar and then said, "At ease, Lethbridge-Stewart. I don't think we have to go quite off the deep end here. Young man . . . you are—?"

"Bhodi Li, sir. And this is Parcival and Tivia."

Churchill looked at the two of them. "Which is which?"

"I'm Tivia," said Parcival.

"I'm Parcival," said Tivia.

"Will you guys quit clowning?" said Bhodi under his breath.

"Young man," said Churchill slowly, "unless I have just gone totally potty—which may be the case—you and your friends just popped out of nowhere into the middle of this room."

Lethbridge-Stewart shook his head. "It was just a trick, Mr. Prime Minister. Had to be. Mass hysteria."

Churchill fixed him with a deadly stare. "Are you implying that I am prone to hysterics, Lethbridge-Stewart?"

"No. No, of course not," he said quickly.

"Excellent. Now that we're agreed that none of us is hysterical—perhaps, young man, you could explain just what in the blazes you are doing here?"

"We've come to warn you!" said Bhodi urgently. "Three monstrous aliens are going to trash your major offensive in just . . . what day is this?"

"It's June 5," said Churchill. "Is that of any significance?"

"Tomorrow! Holy cow, it's tomorrow!"

Churchill's eyes narrowed. "What's tomorrow?"

"It!"

"It what?"

Bhodi looked around desperately for aid. He looked at Parcival who gave him a hi-sign. "You're doing great so far, Bhodi."

"Look," said Bhodi Li desperately. "We're from the

future. We're Photon Warriors. We've come back in time to prevent three minions of the Warlord of Arr from changing history, having Hitler win World War II and then recruiting him as a supporter of the Warlord.''

Churchill stared at him. ''From the future. You're Photon Warriors. Are there any more of you?''

''Oh, yeah,'' said Bhodi quickly. ''There's Leon, who's a giant lizard, and Lord Baethan, who's a cyborg, and Pike, who kind of looks like Mister Potato-head.''

''He does not!'' said Parcival.

''All right, he doesn't. Now clam up.''

The edges of Churchill's mouth turned upward ever so slightly. ''And just how did you come here . . . from the future, you said?''

''Yeah. MOM sent us here.''

And now Churchill laughed outright. ''Did you hear, Lethbridge-Stewart? Their mum sent them. Did she tell you to wear your overcoats because of the London fog?'' He shook his head. ''Look, my friends, you are most intriguing, but I'm afraid that I'm quite busy right now and you will just have to wait until I can attend to you.''

The soldiers started to move forward, and Bhodi shouted, ''Don't you get it? Your men are going to get slaughtered at the big offensive!''

Churchill leaned forward, puffing out smoke from the cigar. ''All right, my boy. If you're from the future, everything we're doing here should be an open book. If we are having a 'major offensive,' where is it going to be?''

Bhodi stood there, flat-footed. He racked his brains. He had been trying to remember all this time. Then what Hitler said came back to him. ''Calais. Someplace named Calais.''

Churchill nodded, cold amusement in his eyes.

And suddenly Bhodi knew that Calais was wrong. That Hitler was wrong. Even as Churchill started to say, ''Take them away,'' Bhodi said, ''Wait! Not Calais. It's . . .''

He banged on the side of his helmet. "Burgundy. Or-mandy." Then his eyes went wide, a mental tumbler clicking into place. "Normandy!"

Churchill put up a hand and the soldiers halted. "What . . . did . . . you . . . say?" Each word was like a rifle shot.

It swept over him like a wave. Everything his grandfather had ever said, burned into his subconscious from the repetition. "Right! Normandy! It was called Operation Fortitude—no! Wait. Operation Fortitude was the program where you encouraged the Nazis to believe that a place called Calais would be where you made your move. You sent out fake radio broadcasts, knowing that the Nazis were tapping in. But the real plan was to invade the beach at Normandy in France, and it was called Overlord."

"Lethbridge-Stewart," said Churchill, "leave the room."

"But—"

"No buts!" It was a voice used to instant obedience. "I said now. Take your men with you."

"Then you'll be alone with them, Mr. Prime Minister! With all due respect . . ."

"Lethbridge-Stewart, I am fully aware of that. But if you want to make yourself useful . . ."

"Yes, sir?"

"Have some tea sent up."

"It was originally going to be June 5," Bhodi said. "Today. But because of awful weather it was pushed back to the 6th."

The three Photon Guardians were seated around a table with Churchill. An elaborate tea cozy sat between them. Bhodi and Parcival were sipping tea, finding it difficult to resist Churchill's invitation. He was particularly solicitous of Tivia, and Bhodi was astonished—if he'd tried to hold Tivia's chair for her so she could sit, she would have broken the chair over his head. Churchill did it and Tivia seemed positively charmed.

She held a cup of tea up to her mouth, realized that the gauze came between the liquid and her, and quietly put the cup back down again.

"You are very educated in these matters, Bhodi Li," said Churchill. "You have information that either someone from the future would have, or the greatest of spies would have. But if you were the greatest of spies, then what in heaven's name would you be doing here? That, combined with your unique method of entrance . . . well, I am reminded of Sherlock Holmes's great precept. When you have eliminated the impossible, then whatever remains, however improbable, must be the truth." He opened an ornate cigar box and extended one to Bhodi.

"No thanks," said Bhodi.

Churchill regarded Parcival and Tivia and obviously dismissed the idea of offering to either of them.

He pulled out a small book of matches as he prepared a new cigar for himself. "So what do you recommend?"

"Put us on the beach with your men. As soon as the Dark Guardians show themselves, we'll take care of them."

Churchill took the cigar between his teeth and started to strike a match. "If they're as threatening as you say . . . are you certain the three of you can handle them?"

Before he could strike the match, a pencil-thin beam of light passed directly in front of him and sizzled off the end of the cigar, neatly lighting it. The Phaser beam continued through the far wall, leaving a small hole.

Churchill looked in astonishment at Bhodi, who was sitting there with his Phaser in his hand. The Photon Warrior looked quite pleased with himself. "I think we can handle it okay," he said.

Tivia sighed. "Please forgive Bhodi, Mr. Prime Minister. He's a bit of a child sometimes."

"That's quite all right," said Churchill.

There was a knock at the door and Lethbridge-Stewart entered. Bhodi gasped as he saw there was now a small, pencil-thin hole drilled through the front of Lethbridge-Stewart's hat.

"Uh-oh," said Parcival.

Lethbridge-Stewart removed his hat and turned it around. An equally small hole protruded from the back, and Bhodi could see the thin line that went straight down the middle of Lethbridge-Stewart's hair from front to back.

Churchill said blandly, "Interesting part in your hair, colonel."

"Everything all right in here, sir?"

"Quite all right. Lethbridge-Stewart . . . get in touch either with Eisenhower or Bradley. Tell them I have to talk to them immediately . . . a matter of vital importance. I'm going to be sky-dropping them three more soldiers."

Lethbridge-Stewart stared at the Photon Warriors, then nodded. "As you wish, sir," and left.

"Hey, I'm really sorry about that," said Bhodi.

Churchill waved it off. "No problem, my boy." There was a pause. "May I ask what you're staring at?"

"Well . . . it's kind of silly," said Bhodi. "But my granddad always said, when I was a baby, I looked like you."

"All babies look like me," said Winston Churchill, and sipped his tea.

16

Blast from the Past

D day, also known as the landing on Normandy, was indeed one of the greatest military coups in history.

Simply put, the Nazis had occupied France, and the allies—the British, Americans, Canadians and so on—had decided that it should be taken back again. The invasion point that was chosen was the French beach of Normandy.

The Germans, although not realizing that an invasion of Normandy would actually take place, had nevertheless heavily fortified the beaches. Among their means of protection were curved steel spears to keep tanks back, armed barriers, giant guns, rockets, infantry traps, tank traps, and concrete bunkers, which were ramparts connected by underground tunnels.

All this was a formidable defense. Even if the allies managed to get on the beaches and not get blown off immediately, they would be fighting their way inland every step of the way. Millions of soldiers were involved.

Yet for all of their defenses, history stated that the Nazis were not able to prevent the allies from taking the beach, from taking the land.

But then, the Nazis previously had not had the three Dark Guardians with them. This time, they did.

The foul weather had cleared up, and now it seemed to Pirarr, looking over the beaches, that there was a hush in the air. Almost as if in anticipation. He looked out over the sea and he saw, far in the distance, the ships approaching. Just as Mandarr had said they would be coming.

Pirarr loved the ocean. He longed to sail it, feel a ship rocking beneath him. Perhaps one day, when the Warlord was supreme, he would be given his own space-spanning ship to command. He would be allowed to loot and pillage to his heart's content. Now that, that was a dream worth fighting to achieve.

He turned on his peg leg and headed inland, towards where he knew his two compatriots would be waiting. They were not in his class, of course. They thought only of serving the Warlord. Their lives were measured in terms of how best it would please the Warlord. The Warlord was the source of all rewards and all punishments, the be-all and the end-all.

Well, that was fine for them. He, Pirarr, wouldn't begrudge them that. But Pirarr had his own wants and desires and if the Warlord wouldn't give them to him, well, then someday he might have to take them.

He was no fool. It was too early to cross swords with the Warlord yet. Warriarr had learned the price of that. But someday. Someday there would come a time, and Pirarr would be ready.

About a mile inland, Mandarr sat perched on a rock, scanning the skies. Destructarr lumbered up to him. "What are you looking for?" demanded the monstrous Dark Guardian. "When do the soldiers come?"

And then Mandarr pointed skyward. "There. The first assault. You see them?"

Destructarr looked up, squinting. "See wh—oh!"

High in the sky, quiet and deadly, the gliders were coming.

The gliders were the first line of attack, an attempt by the allies to cut the German supply lines.

And suddenly the invasion came in force. Paratroopers plummeted from the sky.

Mandarr turned casually to Destructarr. "Care for some target practice, my friend?"

Eagerly Destructarr aimed his arm cannon and began firing at the far-off specks in the sky.

At the same moment rockets from the ground arched upward toward the gliders. And Destructarr, much to Mandarr's dismay, nailed the rockets instead.

"I got it!" exclaimed Destructarr. He turned to Mandarr for approval and Mandarr only grimaced. Before he could stop him, Destructarr called out joyously, "Look! There's more of them!" He fired again and again, picking off German rocket after German rocket until Mandarr grabbed his arm.

Unfortunately he swung Destructarr's arm down at just the wrong time, and the monster blasted a pit right under Mandarr's feet. Mandarr grabbed a tight hold on Destructarr's arm to stop himself from falling in.

"You idiot!" grated Mandarr. "Lift me up!"

Distressed, Destructarr swung his arm around and Mandarr put his feet down on solid ground. He was about to chew out Destructarr but then thought better of it. It was never a particularly good idea to express anger with Destructarr, if it could be at all avoided.

"All right, Destructarr," said Mandarr soothingly. "We'll settle for destroying all the ground troops. For close-up fighting, we'll have them largely all to ourselves."

At that moment Pirarr ran up, waving his sword. "Ahoy, me hearties," he crowed. "We're being boarded."

"Well then," said Mandarr. "Let's prepare to repel boarders, shall we?"

They approached the beach. By now the landing boats had been dispatched. Mandarr watched them come, licking his lips in anticipation.

"We're on the section of beach code-named 'Utah' by the allies," said Mandarr. "Once we've cleaned this section, we'll work our way to Omaha, Gold and the other two. We'll obliterate them to the man, blow their precious tanks out of the water. It will be one of the greatest slaughters in the history of mankind."

"I'm honored," said Pirarr, "to be a part of it."

They watched as the first of the ships, loaded with soldiers, rolled up onto the beach. The huge unloading front of the boat fell open and the soldiers leaped out, hip deep in the water. They looked queasy, even seasick. Mandarr chuckled. "Look at them—they look positively peaked. Let's put them out of their misery, shall we?"

They stepped out from hiding, utterly unafraid. "Destructarr . . . announce us," said Mandarr.

Destructarr aimed his laser cannon and fired.

Down on the beach, a gaping hole now appeared, accompanied by a huge explosion. The air crackled from the force of Destructarr's beam.

Soldiers began to scatter frantically even as a tank rolled out from the boat. It looked like a great hippo rolling through the water, and Pirarr and Mandarr laughed out loud.

"Nail it, Destructarr," said Pirarr.

And then, at the side of the tank, in water that went almost up to his shoulders, there came a small but familiar figure.

Without hesitation Parcival aimed his Phaser and fired.

"No!" screamed Mandarr, and now it was the Dark Guardians who were scattering. The Phaser beam chipped off a chunk of stone behind them.

Only Destructarr was too dumb to run for cover. With a roar the massive Dark Guardian ripped a huge boulder from nearby and turned towards the men who were wading ashore.

Parcival, seeing his opportunity, aimed his Phaser at Destructarr. If Parcival could hit Destructarr's power plate, he knew, it would disrupt the flow of energy with which the Warlord was powering him and would send the Dark Guardian back to his own time. He fired, but Destructarr blocked the shot with the boulder and then, bellowing his defiance, hurled the great rock directly at Parcival and the troops.

Parcival shouted a warning even as he moved to get out of the rock's way. A soldier was right next to Parcival, and directly behind the soldier, trying to get into the fight, was Bhodi Li. Someone from behind Bhodi called out, "Jarvis! Watch it!"

For a split instant Bhodi Li, né Christopher Jarvis, thought that the warning was directed to him. Then he realized that right in front of him was his own grandfather. Even as this became clear to him he knocked his grandfather to the ground, covered him with his own body and turned his Phaser on the flying rock that was now only yards away.

Two Phaser beams joined his as Tivia and Parcival opened fire and the boulder blew up in midair, raining down pebbles and shards of stone.

The young soldier, face down in the beach of Normandy, mumbled to Bhodi, "Would you get off me before you drown me?" Bhodi complied and the soldier sat up.

Bhodi stared into a face not unlike his own, the ears that stuck out even as a young man. Corporal Jarvis said, "I didn't understand at first why the CO sent you three along—although I thought she was good for window dressing." He nodded in Tivia's direction and Bhodi was thankful Tivia hadn't heard the remark. Otherwise he might wind up never being born anyway. Corporal Jarvis continued, "But I'll tell you—I don't know who that freak in the funny suit was, but if he's your problem, more power to you."

Artillery started raining down from the Germans then, and Corporal Jarvis leaped up and joined his squad. Bhodi felt torn for a moment, wanting to follow his grandfather. To protect him. Then he felt Tivia pull at his arm, saying, "Come on. Parcival's way ahead of us. If he takes out all three of them single-handedly, we'll never hear the end of it."

Parcival, meantime, was unaware that his teammates were not close by. He stalked cautiously forward among the rocks farther up the beach, when suddenly a spiked mace swung around out of nowhere. Parcival leaped back but the mace just snagged his hand, knocking his Phaser out of reach. He turned and Destructarr loomed over him.

Parcival backed up quickly, his feet skidding on the soft ground beneath him. He pulled his baseball bat out from his belt and held it firmly by the handle as Pike had taught him to do. Destructarr swung his mace around, the spiked ball whizzing towards Parcival, but with a sweep of his bat Parcival knocked it away. Destructarr bore down on him but Parcival refused to give in to panic, never losing sight of the mace. Keeping his eye on the ball.

Destructarr growled his frustration, raised his arm cannon and fired point-blank. Parcival leaped out of the way and Destructarr shattered more rocks.

Parcival ran, ran as fast as he could. He passed an American soldier who saw him run past, turned and saw what was pursuing the young Photon Guardian. Without hesitation the soldier brought his rifle around and fired point-blank. It bounced off Destructarr's tough hide like marbles. Destructarr turned towards the soldier, growled, "No little human does that to me," and raised his cannon.

"No!" yelled Parcival, and leaping forward, he jammed the end of his baseball bat into Destructarr's cannon. Were Parcival's bat an ordinary Louisville Slugger this would have been a ludicrous move, but it had been given to him by Pike and was made from a special alloy. The result was that when Destructarr fired his cannon, the blast was not able to go out. Unable to release its charge but unable to contain it, Destructarr's beloved arm cannon blew up.

The concussion threw Parcival and the soldier one way, and Destructarr the other. But with hide as tough as a planet, Destructarr recovered first.

Furious, he bore down on a stunned Parcival. He swung his mace high and prepared to smash Parcival's head to pieces.

Meanwhile Bhodi was hunting as well, weaving his way through the maze of rocks and barriers that studded the area. Then he got to the hooks.

They looked like fish hooks lying on the long end, the curved portions projecting into the air. But they were huge, larger than Bhodi was, and made from steel. They were designed to prevent tanks from rolling up off the beach, and they looked like they would do the job.

He sensed it before he saw it, and leaped out of the way of the Phaser blast that would have cut him in two. He somersaulted over the blast right towards Mandarr and fired at the Dark Guardian. But Mandarr, in his previous life the greatest Photon Warrior on earth, was far too quick.

Bhodi fired again, but Mandarr, performing a dazzling series of maneuvers, got in close and with a fierce blow smashed Bhodi on the side of the head. Bhodi dropped his Phaser in the sand, scrambled on hands and knees towards it. But Mandarr was there first and kicked it out of his reach.

"I could have blasted you into atoms from a safe distance, Bhodi Li," howled Mandarr, "but you've been too much trouble, too many times. When I kill you, I want to do it firsthand!" He grabbed Bhodi by the front of his armor and started to shove him backward, and Bhodi knew with horror what Mandarr's intention was. He was going to slam the helpless Warrior back against one of the upright hooks. If they were meant to stop tanks, they could certainly put an end to Bhodi Li.

Desperately Bhodi kicked Mandarr in the stomach. The move caught Mandarr off guard and he dropped Bhodi, gasping for breath. Bhodi swung a right to Mandarr's solar plexus, but Mandarr caught it, grabbed Bhodi and twisted him around. Bhodi gritted his teeth against the pain, forced the fear away and slammed down on Mandarr's instep. For a second Mandarr released his hold, and Bhodi reached around, put a hammerlock around Mandarr's neck and tossed him in a perfect judo throw.

Mandarr hit the ground but caught the impact on his shoulders and forearms. Before Bhodi realized what was happening, Mandarr, upside down, delivered a sharp kick to the front of Bhodi's helmet. The face visor protected him from the full impact but it still staggered him. Before he could recover, Mandarr was on his feet.

This time the Dark Guardian did not let up. He battered poor Bhodi repeatedly in the stomach, in the chest. Bhodi weakly tried to put up a defense, but Mandarr drove him back, back. Bhodi blocked one punch to the head but before he could counterpunch, Mandarr kneed him in the stomach. Bhodi choked and fought back, but he had never managed to beat Mandarr in hand-to-hand before, and it didn't seem that he was going to be able to beat him this time. And there might not be another chance.

Bhodi's foot hit something metal and he realized that Mandarr had pushed him all the way back to the hook. He grabbed at Mandarr desperately, and Mandarr laughed, exerting his strength slowly, slowly, savoring the moment. One of Bhodi's hands grabbed at Mandarr's chest, the other at his waist, trying to find a firm hold, but Mandarr wasn't going to let it happen. With a grin he shoved Bhodi up and back, and although they were still chest-too-chest, Bhodi felt the edge of the hook poking against his back.

"You're finished, Bhodi Li," snarled Mandarr. "At long last. There's no way out. You're too weak to beat me man-to-man. None of your precious fellow Guardians are around to shoot at the power plate on my chest. And you—you don't even have your Phaser.''

Suddenly Bhodi stopped struggling and, as Mandarr prepared to ram him through the hook, Bhodi grated through clenched teeth, ''There's one thing I do have.''

Intrigued, Mandarr stopped for just a moment. ''Really? What might that be?''

''*Your* Phaser!''

Mandarr looked down. He had been so intent on impaling Bhodi on the hook that he hadn't realized that Bhodi had pulled Mandarr's Phaser out of its holster.

He tried to shove Bhodi onto the hook but it was too late. Point-blank Bhodi fired on Mandarr's chest plate. With a scream Mandarr staggered back, clutching at the plate even as he felt the atoms of his body disassembling, being yanked back into his own time.

''My own weapon!'' he howled. ''It's not fair! *It's not fair*!'' And with that final protest he was slingshot back to the future.

Bhodi, who had fallen to the ground when Mandarr released him, dusted himself off, found his Phaser and went in search of his allies.

Parcival, in the meantime, saw his death descending towards him.

As Destructarr bore down on him, swinging his mace, Parcival knew that he wouldn't have the strength to deflect it. The smoking ruin of the cannon on Destructarr's arm gave him little comfort in what seemed to be his final moment.

And at that instant, with a whizzing sound like a horde of bees, a star blade shot across the air and hit Destructarr's chest plate.

He staggered back and watched in bewilderment as his arms began to discorporate. By the time he figured out what was happening, the rest of him had followed.

The American soldier stared at Parcival, at Tivia who had just come up behind Parcival, and at the place where

Destructarr had been. Then he shook his head, said, "I'm sorry, but this is too weird for me. I'm leaving." And, good to his word, he took off.

Parcival looked down. A hand grenade had come loose from the soldier's belt. For a moment he was jolted, but then he saw that the pin was still in place. He picked it up and studied it. "Fascinating device."

Then Tivia's ears pricked up as she heard a scrape of metal on stone. Pirarr had a peg leg made of metal, which meant—

"Parcival, watch out!"

From behind cover, Pirarr brought his sword gun to bear. It was shaped like a cutlass, but the hilt was a trigger and energy blasts leaped from the tip of the blade.

Parcival jumped in front of Tivia, took a stance with his bat, and as Pirarr fired, he expertly deflected each of the shots with the bat. Pirarr cursed under his breath and ducked away, hoping to find a more advantageous position.

Parcival grinned. "Luke Skywalker, eat your heart out."

"Who?" asked Tivia. "Is he a Photon Warrior?"

"Not exactly. Come on."

They approached Pirarr's hiding place from separate sides, not realizing that Pirarr had already changed position. Moving with exceptional swiftness for someone with one false leg, Pirarr had maneuvered his way around the Photon Guardians, and now with an expectant sneer he raised his weapon and aimed at their unprotected backs.

That was when he felt the business end of a Phaser pressed against his head.

Bhodi Li said, "Don't tell me you're the type of person who would shoot people in the back."

Pirarr swung his leg around and fired directly at Bhodi's feet. Bhodi had forgotten that Pirarr's peg leg doubled as a laser, and he cursed himself out even as he backflipped out of the way.

The movement caught Tivia and Parcival's attention.

Even as Pirarr fled, the three Photon Guardians went after him in hot pursuit.

Pirarr ran, ran as fast as his considerable bulk would allow him. He kept looking behind him and, as the Photon Warriors closed on him, he fired wildly with his sword gun. He didn't even come close to hitting them.

Tivia paused a moment and hurled a star blade. Pirarr, with a lot of luck, shot the star blade in midair and it fell to the ground.

Pirarr, looking back over his shoulder, chortled at his good fortune. This was about two seconds before he fell into the pit.

He tumbled heels over head into the deep hole which Destructarr had so conveniently blasted into the ground earlier. It was about seven feet deep and, falling head first, Pirarr landed on his back, his legs in the air. He scrambled and twisted around and by the time he had gotten to his feet, the pit was surrounded by Photon Warriors.

"Oh, Pirarr," Tivia called sweetly. He turned to see that she had taken the grenade from Parcival and pulled the pin. She hurled it with the same casual accuracy she used with her star blades, and the grenade lodged itself firmly in the open mouth of the fake serpent that twined around Pirarr's shoulders. "A gift to the Warlord. Gift wrap him, Bhodi."

Bhodi fired a single shot at Pirarr's chest plate and the pirate immediately rebounded to his own time.

The Guardians looked at each other and grinned. "Do you think the Warlord will like our gift?" asked Tivia.

Bhodi could barely suppress a laugh. "Well, I'll say one thing—if he doesn't, he sure isn't going to be able to return it."

Pirarr materialized on the Warlord's time platform. Had he been paying attention he would have been surprised to see Destructarr and Mandarr already there. But he wasn't paying attention—he was busy pulling frantically at the live hand grenade in the mouth of his snake.

The grenade came loose and, dropping it to the platform, Pirarr ran and yelled "Run! It's going to go—"

The grenade exploded. Circuitry fried and energy crackled through the throne room of the Warlord of Arr. The Warlord screamed as his time platform, the platform that had taken so much energy and time to create, disappeared in a shower of sparks and burning mechanisms. The sound of the explosion reverberated throughout the Warlord's base. And even when the explosion died down, the Warlord's howls of fury continued unabated for some time.

Pirarr, Mandarr and Destructarr stood trembling in front of their master, and eventually his screams died down. Then there was nothing. He just stared at him from deep inside the darkness, his glowing eyes taking them in. Pirarr gulped and Mandarr managed to stammer out, "My Lord. My Lord, we are sorry."

There was a moment's pause, and then the Warlord's voice sounded, low and heavy. "Yes. Yes, I'm sure you are."

They breathed a sigh of relief.

"And I," continued the Warlord. "I am sorry for you, too. Come here."

They began to tremble. "No my Lord. Please," stammered Mandarr. "We'll do better next time. We will."

"Yes," intoned the Warlord. "I know you will. I said . . . come here."

His huge clawed hand, dripping with hideous liquid, reached out of the darkness towards them.

And the screaming did not stop again for quite some time.

17

For the Glory

"So, Bhodi Li, you had your first real experience with a full-scale war. Glorious, isn't it?"

Leon was chortling in his gravelly voice and patted him on the back so hard that he almost dislocated Bhodi's shoulder. "I've been in more wars than I can count. Fought my way from Alpha Centauri to Zeta Minor. And it's always the same. Glorious. Makes life worth living."

"I don't know, Leon," said Bhodi, removing his helmet and sitting back in one of the spare rooms of Intellistar. After a particularly harrowing adventure, he liked to take an hour or so to recuperate before returning to Earth. "Fighting with other humans, real bullets . . . it all felt so weird. I don't know how you do it."

"It's the greatest thing in the known cosmos," declared Leon. "Why, we old soldiers just love to tell war stories. You want to hear some of the best?"

"Well, actually . . ."

"Good." Leon plopped down next to him. "My first campaign was on the planet Goodwin. There was a horde of raging Duffys heading my way, but did Leon flinch? Did Leon run?''

Did Bhodi care? thought Bhodi.

He started to screen out what Leon was saying, thinking about all that had happened to him in the past—

The past! It hit him like a thunderbolt. Here he had gotten into all this trouble because he had refused to be interested in the experiences of others. And now he was doing it all over again. "Leon," he said quickly. "I'm sorry. I was distracted. Could you start over?"

"Start over?" The huge lizard looked at him quizzically.

"Yeah. I don't want to miss anything. I might be able to use some of your tactics myself."

Leon tilted his head back and laughed—actually Leon didn't laugh so much as explode with amusement. "Now, that's the kind of attitude I like. Someone who's willing to learn. Not like that Tivia. She's an incredible female, but if you're a male, she's not the least bit interested in what you have to say."

Slowly Bhodi shook his head. "Oh, I don't know about that. In fact, I wouldn't say that at all."

"You had to make yourselves up?" asked Pike.

He and Baethan were talking with Parcival and Tivia. Pike shook his head. "How depressing. It's a shame I didn't go." And with a thought he suddenly was a perfect human, with blond hair and blue eyes.

"And I," rumbled Baethan, "could have used my magic to disguise your appearance in a more efficient fashion. MOM"—and he turned to the flickering image on the wall—"may I ask why you chose the particular personnel that you did?"

MOM's dulcet tones echoed through the room. "The selection of Bhodi, Tivia and Parcival was logical since they were all humanoid and therefore could most easily fit in in terms of appearance and behavior."

"But they still stood out," said Pike, who had reverted to his normal appearance.

Imperturbably, MOM replied, "Obviously this was not an overwhelming handicap since the mission was accomplished. You may all return to your respective planets now."

They looked at each other, mildly surprised. MOM didn't usually dismiss them in that manner, but they shrugged it off. They had come to think of MOM as more human than computer, and so had no difficulty thinking of her as someone capable of being moody.

And so, one by one, the Photon Guardians left Intellistar. This time around Parcival went back with Pike instead of hanging out at Intellistar, since Pike had become virtually a father to him anyway.

Always the last to arrive, Bhodi was the last to leave as well. And as he was transformed into the energy particles that would be shot back to Earth, he thought he noted something wrong. Were MOM's lights flickering just a little differently, just slightly off-color? He shrugged it off. MOM was MOM. She was the first Photon Guardian, and she had always been, and she always would be. Without her there would be no Photon Warriors. She was a constant.

It was an attitude that all the Photon Guardians shared.

And eventually it would prove to be a mistake.

Christopher Jarvis rematerialized in the Photon Center and completed his game. As always he proved untouchable by others, but flawlessly managed to rack up his own score as he nailed player after player.

When the six minutes were up, Chris walked quickly out of the arena and hung up his helmet and gear. Other players were lingering in the ready area and said, "Chris! Only one game? We need you, man." And the members of the opposing team echoed the sentiments, but only because they wanted a chance to get even.

Chris waved them off. "Sorry, guys, I gotta head home. My grandpa's visiting and I have to get back."

"Aw, man, my condolences," said Dexter, who went by the fighting name of Ace.

"No, it's okay. He's an okay guy. You know he was there when the allies landed at Normandy?"

Dexter stared at him. "Landed at Normandy? What's that, like an airport or something?"

Chris shook his head. "Man, you don't know from nothing." He turned and dashed out of the Photon Center, leaped onto his bike and pedaled for home as fast as he could.

When he got there, he strode in the door and trotted up to the guest room, where his grandfather stayed. To his surprise he saw Grandpa Lou was packing his small suitcase. "Where you going, Grandpa?"

Lou turned to him and there was a bit of sadness in his eyes. "I'm going home, Christopher. I've come to the realization that I'm just in the way around here. You all have your own lives to live and you don't need an old man hanging around." He snapped the suitcase shut and picked it up. "I'll see you around Christmas time."

In no uncertain terms Chris took the suitcase from him and placed it on the bed. "You're not leaving, Grandpa."

Lou looked at him uncertainly. "I'm not?"

"You're not." He sat down. "Grandpa, I want to apologize. I've been doing a lot of running around and I haven't really been paying too much attention to everything that you've been telling me. It's because the past has always seemed dead and uninteresting to me. But it doesn't have to be that way."

Lou grinned. "Well, it's never been to me."

"Because not only is it interesting to know what's gone before, but it can have real applications to what's going on now."

"Well," said Lou. "I think you really mean that."

"I do." Chris grinned and saw for a moment that young

soldier in his Grandpa's face. He was only a couple of years older than Chris himself. Wouldn't it be something if everybody could see their folks at an easier age to relate to?

"Well, you know, Christopher," Lou was saying, "it's probably my fault to some extent. All I've been doing is repeating the same old stories to you. It means I have to do one of several things. Either I have to come up with new stories, or begin making them up."

As Chris laughed, Grandpa Lou raised a finger. "I do have something new, now that I think about it. While cleaning out my attic the other day, I found some really old photos. They're here in my suitcase. You know, when I was your age, I even looked a lot like you. Although when you were a baby you looked like Churchill."

"Eh," said Chris. "All babies look like Churchill."

"Yes, that's . . ." He paused. "That's true. You say it like you actually heard of Churchill."

"Of course," said Chris. "I've heard of lots of stuff. Although I still find the most interesting part of World War II to be D day. That was something, huh?"

"Yes. Although . . ." And now he frowned. "There was so much going on that it's hard to remember it as much more than a jumble of images. But you know . . . I seem to remember a giant boulder flying at me. Isn't that strange?"

"Strange," agreed Chris.

"Well," shrugged Grandpa. "At any rate, here are the pictures. I don't think you've ever seen such old pictures. I was never much at saving these kinds of things. Your grandmother was the real nostalgist of the two of us. She never threw out anything."

Chris took a stack of brittle black and white pictures that his grandfather handed him. There were several photos of his grandfather in his uniform and then in an outrageous-looking civilian uniform.

He flipped to the next picture and stopped dead.

"Why, Christopher," his grandfather said, seeing his expression. "What in the world is the matter?"

He pointed. "This woman. Who is this?"

"That's your Grandma Sarah, of course."

He blinked, never having seen a picture of his grandmother so young. "Sarah. Not Gretta, then."

"Why, yes," said Grandpa Lou in surprise. "I don't recall ever mentioning that to you. When I met her, her name was Gretta Sarah Meuller." He sighed wistfully. "I never liked the name Gretta, so she had me call her by her middle name. It was my pet name for her. And you know, she had a pet name for me. I never told anyone. Would you like to know what it was?"

Feeling numb, Chris said hollowly, "Sure, Grandpa."

"Boaty. She never told me why. I always assumed it was because I liked boats so much." He shook his head. "Lovely woman, your grandmother. Brave as anything, too. I met her after the war, you know."

"Yes. I know." He stared at the picture and smiled. Then he kissed the tip of his finger and placed it against her cheek. "Gretta. She looks so happy here. And yet, somehow . . ."

Grandpa Lou nodded. "There was always just a touch of melancholy about her. I'm not surprised, considering everything she lost. She was a German refugee, you know. I was never really clear on how she got out, except that she came to this country late in 1944. Odd, isn't it? I was getting into Europe and she was getting out at the same time."

"Yeah. Wild."

"Lovely woman, Christopher. A shame she died when you were only three. So you don't remember her really. You would have liked her a lot."

"Yeah," said Chris. "You're right, Grandpa. I probably would have liked her. A lot."

Also Available:

Meet the newest Photon
Warrior—Gambler. Will he
be the greatest help the
Photon Guardians have
ever known . . . or the
greatest threat? Plus the
mystery of MOM deepens.
All in

PHOTON #2: HIGH STAKES

The Light Shines!